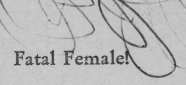

Fatal Female!

Darlene whipped around, her eyes blazing, her lips like a red gash on her face. "You bastard! You killed him! You killed him!"

Darlene brought her gun around and fired. Harry turned aside, narrowly missing the bullet meant for him. There was another shot. But this one came from an altogether new direction. And found a completely unexpected target. . . .

Books by Dane Hartman

Dirty Harry #1: Duel For Cannons
Dirty Harry #2: Death on the Docks

Published by
WARNER BOOKS

DIRTY HARRY #2

Death on the Docks

Dane Hartman

WARNER BOOKS

A Warner Communications Company

DIRTY HARRY #2

Death on the Docks

The Beginning . . .

It was way past midnight when the blue Dodge convertible belonging to Bernard Tuber pulled into his driveway. There was just one light left on in the house—in the front hall—so that Tuber wouldn't have to fumble around looking for a switch. The shades were drawn in the upstairs windows; Marianne and the children were asleep.

For nearly half a minute Tuber and Halsey, his bodyguard, waited in the car. They did this by force of habit. If either of them sensed anything was wrong, Tuber would simply start the ignition and race back down the driveway. It had been like this since the onset of the election campaign for Local 242 of the Brotherhood of Longshoremen. It wouldn't have been so bad if Bernard Tuber had been given little chance of winning. The problem was that he had every prospect of being victorious in the election the following day.

He was a quiet, reflective man; you looked at him and you figured he was a professor of anthropology at nearby Stanford University. You didn't take him for a former stevedore who twice had nearly lost his life on the docks. He didn't appear to be very strong, but he was; more than muscle he had the will and stamina to try and wrest control of the union from Matt Braxton's machine.

But will wasn't enough. Not when you began getting obscene phone calls threatening the lives of you and your

7

family; not when prowlers hurled rocks through your picture window in the middle of the night. You needed more than will then. You needed somebody like Halsey, a man who knew how to use a .357 Magnum and when to use it.

Halsey was big, football big and basketball tall, and when he stepped out of the car and took up position astride Tuber he loomed over his boss by nearly a foot.

"Something's wrong," Tuber said, gazing out at the street. "I'm not sure what it is but I can smell it."

Halsey's eyes were working furiously to determine what it was.

"Streetlight's out," he noted.

The light that should have illuminated the sidewalk and lawn was not there. The only available light was coming from the lamp Marianne had left on.

"Of course, it could be that the bulb failed," Tuber said dubiously. "It happens."

"You want to go back to the car?"

They were already approaching the winding paved walkway that led to the door.

"No, no, it makes no sense to do that. Nothing else seems wrong."

He was right; except for the monotonous chirping of crickets and the occasional sound of a car passing in the distance, there was nothing to disturb the air of tranquillity.

The two men advanced quickly. Not running, nothing to show panic, but a well-paced step that got them up to the handsome white door where they stood out starkly in the lamplight.

To either side of the door there were bushes that rose waist-high; they were thick but manicured, a nice suburban touch.

It was a sudden rustling in the bushes on his right side that caused Halsey to turn abruptly in that direction. At the same time, instinctively, he brought his .357 into view.

Tuber, his key already in the door, looked blankly at

Halsey. He'd had little sleep in the last few weeks and tonight he'd had to endure a final strategy session that had gone on interminably. His reaction speed wasn't as good as it should have been.

"I don't know," Halsey started to say when there was a roar from the left, from the bushes over on that side. Halsey, his chest torn open by the blast of a shotgun, pitched over backward, smacking his skull hard against the cement walkway. The fractured skull was gratuitous; he was already dead.

Tuber scarcely had a chance to react. Two men wearing ski masks had risen from the right, another—the one who'd just killed Halsey—emerged on the left, all brandishing shotguns. They seemed to wait—not long, a second, two seconds maybe, just long enough for Tuber to realize his fate. Still he struggled with the key, succeeding in opening the door just as all three men fired their weapons, as if on cue. One blast threw Tuber forward, another back, and so for the briefest time he seemed to be suspended in midair, a corpse even before he landed, without a face, without a chest, without a stomach. Blood spouted into the air in grotesque mimicry of a geiser. Then, inevitably, he came down, crashing against the splintered door he'd just opened and toppling into his carpeted foyer.

"What is going on?"

Marianne's hysterical voice carried down to the assailants. They stepped into the foyer, raising their guns just as Tuber's wife, a modestly attractive woman in a red flannel robe, came down the stairs.

Seeing the men, malignant figures in blue ski masks, their clothing spattered with blood, then spotting her husband's body sprawled out beneath them, she tried to scream. Couldn't. No sound at all emerged from her lips.

Her face had paled, her hands trembled noticeably by her sides, and her eyes had gone as wide as they could. It was the moment when everything changes with no warning. No time to build up to it, no time to prepare. It's

9

the suddenness of it that gets people. And it's that moment that the three men in the foyer savored most of all. They were very still, just waiting for her to do something. The way they were acting it was as if they had all the time in the world.

Right then she thought of her children. That spurred her to action. She turned and in her haste almost tripped, then she started to scamper up the stairs. The first blast took her head almost clean off. The body had some momentum and kept on for another step while the head, with its thick crest of brunette hair, swayed precariously on the stump of her neck. Then she collapsed, tumbling clumsily down the stairs, but so rapidly that the gunmen were forced to step out of the way for her. She came to rest on top of her husband's prostrate form.

It should have been enough. It wasn't. The men made their way up the bloodsoaked stairs. At the top two more victims were waiting for them, a six-year-old boy and a three-year-old girl. The six-year-old was out on the landing, screaming in terror, clutching his teddybear close to his chest, his eyes blinded by tears.

"Hey, kid, what are you bawling for? There's nothing to cry about."

The gunman, with his gloved hands, carefully put down the shotgun. This gesture, however, did nothing to reassure the child. Nor should it have. For the assassin now had a Browning automatic gripped in his right hand; he pointed it straight down so that it touched the little boy's scalp and discharged it. The head seemed to explode; flesh and agglutinative gray matter and blood spattered over the walls.

Retrieving the shotgun, the gunman now proceeded into the children's bedroom. Sighting the rifle on the crib in front of him, he fired. The crib and the three-year-old girl lying in it disappeared for a moment in a cloud of smoke and splinters. When it became visible again, the gunman could see that he had failed to hit the girl. Not that it made any difference. A slice of wood, shaven off the crib by the blast, had come down on the sleeping girl

10

like a dagger, impaling her to what was left of the mattress.

The three assailants now left, hastily but not in panic, more like guests who'd lingered too long at a party than murderers who'd left behind four corpses—all that remained of Bernard Tuber and his family.

One

The phone rang. At first it was not clear to Harry that the insistent ringing was not part of his dream. From his bed he groped for the evil instrument, and then remembered that it was his day off and that there was no compelling reason to answer the phone. The hell with it, he thought, let it ring.

And it rang. And it rang. Whoever was on the other end had a good idea that Harry was home and was not about to give up. Finally, unable to stand it any longer, Harry surrendered.

"Callahan."

"Harry? Can you get down here right away?"

Lieutenant Bressler did not need to introduce himself; his voice was immediately—and painfully—recognizable to Harry.

"You got the wrong man, Lieutenant. You forget, it's my day off."

"It used to be your day off. Don't worry, we'll make it up to you. Someday. It's important, Harry."

"Is this an order you're giving me?"

"Think of it as a personal favor." With that Bressler hung up.

"Personal favor, shit," muttered Harry as he sat up in bed, wondering just how he was to get a handle on the coming day. And God knows, there was a lot of the day to come: it was only six-thirty in the morning.

The phone rang again.

"Callahan."

"Harry, this is DiGeorgio. The lieutenant says to tell you to make sure you pick up a paper on the way to work."

"What's he going to do, test me for my knowledge of current events?"

"Front page, Harry. That's all you have to know."

"Tell him he owes me twenty cents then. And the day."

MASSACRE IN PALO ALTO
Tuber, Wife, Kids Shot
Union Elections Postponed

Harry scanned the *Chronicle*'s coverage of the slayings; it went on for pages. Nothing like a juicy bit of mayhem to get the adrenalin rushing in a jaded reporter, he thought.

The paper folded in his hand, Harry strode through the station house which smelled like stale cigarette smoke, stale coffee, and stale sweat. No one looked particularly awake, neither the officers who were getting off nor the ones who were just coming on duty.

DiGeorgio was tapping out a report on a cranky old typewriter. He glanced up as Harry passed. Observing that he'd picked up a copy of the paper he said, "It's a shitty business, Harry. Two kids. Adults, that's one thing. Kids. What kind of son of a bitch blows defenseless kids away?"

Harry just shook his head. He didn't want any part of it. It was his day off, or it used to be, and the killings took place in Palo Alto. This was San Francisco.

Bressler had a succinct enough explanation. "You're being lent out, Harry." He was pacing back and forth behind his desk. He, too, appeared fatigued. Harry could sense when the lieutenant was about to snap; you could see it in his eyes, there was a real coldness there, absolute zero coldness. He didn't like Harry, and yet usually he could keep his distaste for him under control. But when the lieutenant got like this, frazzled, worn down, that control slipped away.

"Mind telling me why I'm the lucky one?"

"Let's just say it's your type of case. Sick, scummy, dirty."

"And political?"

"Who said anything about politics?"

"Tuber was a dissident. He opposed Braxton and Braxton's handpicked candidate Ryan. He was going to win."

"That's speculation. Who knows who would've won. That's not your concern."

"Oh, I don't know, Lieutenant. Suppose it was Braxton who ordered the hit, you think you're going to put the darling of every politician and bureaucrat in this state behind bars?"

Bressler pretended to ignore him. "You seen this?" He indicated a column on the front page of the *Chronicle* that Harry had already read. That didn't stop Bressler; he insisted on reading it aloud: " 'Matthew Braxton, retiring president of Local 242 of the Brotherhood of Longshoremen, when informed of the murders, said that he was "anguished and shocked beyond description," adding that he "would do all in my power to see to the arrest and conviction of the perpetrators of this horrible outrage." To that end, he has instructed the union to put up a fifty thousand dollar reward for information leading to—' "

"I get the picture, Lieutenant. But as far as I'm concerned, it doesn't mean shit."

"They're expecting you in Palo Alto, Harry. I've told them you're on your way. The man you see there is Redhorn. Captain Redhorn."

"Got it."

Redhorn would have made a terrific tour guide He had a face for poker games and a mind for computer

14

chess. He escorted Harry through the Tuber house as though he'd been doing it for the last twenty-two years. Everywhere Harry looked members of the Palo Alto force were exploring for evidence. There were ballistics people and homicide people and forensics people. What the hell did they need him for?

The Tuber house, in fact, could have been some ancient archaeological site the way investigators were poring over it. Flashbulbs were popping furiously as police photographers sought to record every possible nook and cranny. Specialists were down on their hands and knees with knives, shredding flakes of dried blood into plastic envelopes which were then labeled and sealed. Others were gouging out chunks of the walls in which bullets were embedded.

"We've questioned the neighbors," Redhorn was saying. "An elderly couple across the street say they heard some noises around midnight, but they apparently didn't get out of bed to see what it was. The problem is that this house is located way at the end of the street. As you probably saw when you got here there's nothing behind the house. Just woods. As for the house right next door, it's up for sale so no one's in it."

"No witnesses," Harry said, "and no suspects."

"You're jumping to conclusions." Redhorn was guiding Harry up the stairs which were now naked wood, the bloodied carpet having been stripped completely and sent down to the Chem-Toxicology lab for analysis. "While we don't have any suspects yet we're waiting word from PATRIC. PATRIC hasn't failed me yet."

PATRIC, Harry remembered, was an acronym for a computer system called Pattern Recognition and Information Correlations. The system contained a vast bank of data on known criminals, MOs, outstanding warrants, stolen vehicles, rap sheets, field reports. If it was fed the right sort of information, in twenty minutes it could come back with a list of possible suspects. But this was not a case where PATRIC could be of any help.

"The fucking people who did this," Harry said, starting grimly at the jagged stain the six-year-old's blood had made on the wall, "are professionals."

"Professionals!" Redhorn scoffed, looking at Harry, probably wondering why they sent somebody like him from the San Francisco office. "Professionals do a much cleaner job. And they don't generally do a number on kids. It's my opinion that this is the work of psychopaths, raving lunatics—maybe high on drugs."

"You don't think it has anything to do with the union?"

"The union, the union. That's all I ever hear about. This morning when I get here the press is outside screaming about the union. What do I know from unions?"

Harry understood that in this Palo Alto captain he was not about to discover an ally.

"I don't know what else I can tell you. Once we get the results back from ballistics and the serology report we'll let you know. And I'll get a copy of the field report to you."

"And PATRIC? I'd like to hear what PATRIC has to say."

Redhorn didn't catch the mockery in Harry's voice. "Oh sure. Absolutely. Fuck-ups who pull this kind of thing, they should stick out like a sore thumb. PATRIC should pick them up pretty quickly."

PATRIC didn't pick up shit, of course. Serology reports showed only blood from the victims was present on the site and none from any perpetrator. The ballistics report revealed that the bullet that had killed Tuber's son was a 9mm Parabellum cartridge. Otherwise, all the bullets were 2¾-inch, 12-gauge shotshells, fired from Kawaguchiya M-250 autoloading shotguns. The Kawaguchiya, imported through a marketing firm in Tucson, was something of a newcomer to the country. It was hoped that the ones used to murder the Tubers wouldn't be too difficult to trace. Harry knew better. They'd never find them. It wouldn't surprise him if the shotguns were back

16

in Japan; who knows, maybe some clowns were using them right now to hold up a Tokyo bank or blast one another away on the Ginza.

In any case, Harry wasn't convinced that finding the hit men was the most important part of this case. The hit men were only flunkies, probably imported like the Kawaguchiyas they used. But the man who had employed them, for all his protestations of innocence, that man was right here in San Francisco. Matt Braxton.

Two

"Dorothy, show Mr. Callahan in." The voice that came through the intercom was booming. Whoever owned that voice was not a man to be trifled with.

Dorothy had nice long legs, delectably revealed by a seemingly endless split in her skirt. Harry didn't mind following her at all.

The offices of the Brotherhood were spacious, airy, with picture windows yielding splendid panoramas of the Embarcadero and the sparkling blue waters of the bay. The most striking object in the room into which Harry was brought was the desk. It was low and lean and dominated the room and, like all the rest of the furniture, it was Swedish Modern, very tasteful.

The man who sat behind this desk didn't look like he fit in very well with the decor. He was a big, bulky specimen of humanity who seemed to have had to squash himself to get into his chair. One look at his rough-hewn face, with crags and juttings that could have been pilfered from the Grand Canyon, and you had a good idea why he was known as Bull. John "Bull" Ryan. The man who would be king. Well, not king, but president of the Brotherhood. Which was one hell of a lot of power for a man to wield.

Bull was doing his utmost to appear dignified. But he didn't seem to find his pinstriped jacket and indigo tie any more comfortable than his Swedish Modern chair.

18

Papers were strewn over his vast desk, and there was a telephone with half a dozen extensions, all of which were lit up when Harry walked in.

Bull stood up, and leaning across his desk, he grasped hold of Harry's hand. His was a grip that could turn a man's fingers to the consistency of gum.

He motioned for Harry to sit. He sat himself, muttering, "A terrible thing, a terrible thing about poor Bernie and his family," wanting to get a head start on the business at hand. "This is a blot upon our union." His voice was thick and hoarse, possibly from the cigarettes he kept lighting up and then, a minute or so later, jabbing out in the cluttered ashtray. "Keep trying to quit," he said. "I try these low tar things. Low tar's for shit." He slouched back. "So ask away. That's what you came here for, isn't it?"

"When did you last see the deceased?"

"Bernie? A few weeks ago. At a rally he was given. I just happened to stop by. I was interested in his campaigning strategy. As his rival, you know, I was naturally curious to see what he was saying."

"And what was he saying, Mr. Ryan?"

"Bull, please. Everybody calls me Bull. Well, he was saying some very nasty things. Malicious statements. No basis in fact. But, hey, you shouldn't talk mean of the dead, right? Bernie was, shall we say, misguided? Accusing my predecessor and myself of corrupt practices, of stealing union funds for our own personal use." Bull shook his head gravely.

"By predecessor you mean, I take it, Mr. Braxton?"

"Matt, of course, Matt. I tell you something, Mr. Callahan. Matt Braxton worked and slaved all his life for this union. The police—excuse me for saying this—the police worked him over in the old days. You can't count the times Matt got his head bashed in on picket lines. And to accuse this fine individual of stealing from the very men he fought for! It's an outrage."

"So was what happened to Tuber and his family," Harry remarked dryly.

"Of course. Life's an outrage when you think about it."

"Do you have any suspicions about who might have been responsible?"

"Jesus, I wish I did. Our union has put up fifty thousand dollars, you know. We're as interested in apprehending the killers as you people are."

This was an answer that Harry had anticipated. He realized he was only going to be wasting his time if he persisted in questioning Bull. Bull was in any case a mouthpiece. He would say whatever Braxton wanted him to say.

"Do you think you could arrange for me to meet Mr. Braxton?"

"Well, Mr. Braxton's a very busy man. Speaking engagements all over the state. This morning he had to go down to Sacramento to meet with the Governor."

"I can appreciate Mr. Braxton's heavy schedule but all the same I would like to talk to him."

"Of course. I'll speak to his secretary and we'll set up something for you in the very near future."

"Make it soon," said Harry as he rose to leave. "I'm a very impatient man."

As soon as Harry had left, Bull instructed Dorothy to put him in touch with Braxton at his hotel suite in Sacramento.

"I was just going out the door," Braxton said, sounding irritated at having been disturbed. "What is it, Bull?"

"I just had a cop in here, name of Callahan, Harry Callahan. Questioning me on the Tuber thing."

"That's to be expected. Is that why you called me?"

"Well, I wanted to know if we should expect any trouble."

"From the cops? Hey, look, Bull, this is Matt Braxton you're talking to. Nobody's about to touch Matt Braxton."

Bull was wondering whether this insurance extended to him as well but decided not to ask. "This Callahan fellow wants to talk to you."

"So let him talk, what the hell do I care? Bull, if you're so goddamn worried about him put somebody on him. I'm telling you though there's nothing to worry about. Now I really got to get going here. Mustn't keep the Governor waiting."

Even a small matter like ordering surveillance on a lone inspector of the San Francisco Police Department was nothing that Bull could determine without word from Braxton. That was exactly why he was Braxton's hand-picked candidate. He was the next best thing to a marionette.

Half an hour after a man had been put on his tail Harry was aware of him. Harry actually felt him before he saw him. It was a sixth sense he had, honed after too many years on the force. An eye in the back of his head would have served him no better.

When he glimpsed him, it was from half a block away. The tail was a creature made for anonymity; of average height and weight, he could have passed for a bank teller, an insurance salesman, a bureaucrat sapped of life and humanity, the sort that could lose himself on Main Street in a ghost town. Harry knew his kind. You lost sight of him and the next thing you knew he was putting a gun to your skull and blowing out its contents.

But Harry also realized that the tail was not about to take any kind of major action. He was just checking Harry out, probably keeping a record of what he was doing, where he was going.

Where he was going now was to a Chinese restaurant on Spofford Street, in the heart of Old Chinatown. He was hungry and in the mood for the Szechuan food the Quemoy Inn was noted for: hot and spicy enough to cry over. In fact, you ate enough of it you had no choice but to start crying.

The tail was having none of it. He lingered on the corner opposite the restaurant. Every so often Harry would part the luridly red bamboo shades and see him there, studying the *Chronicle* with the intensity of a scholar. People like that had to have the patience of Methuselah waiting to die. Hell, Harry thought, let him wait. He was in no particular hurry.

Harry had just gotten through his hot-and-sour soup, savoring the burning sensation it induced in his mouth, when a couple of youths sauntered into the Quemoy; like virtually all of the other customers they were Chinese. They looked hungry all right, but not for food. Their eyes were skillful, taking everything in at once. Obviously searching for somebody. And even though there were a great many people in the place, noisily going about the business of eating, the two newcomers had little difficulty in finding who it was they were looking for. And finding their subject they wasted little time in removing 9mm Double Action handguns from underneath their jackets and leveling at him.

Being too preoccupied with protecting himself at the moment, Harry couldn't figure out whether they intended to open fire on just one individual or a mixed assortment. Didn't matter. He had already dropped out of his chair and proceeded to shove over his table, knocking the beef dish he had looked forward to eating to the floor.

The two youths—they couldn't have more than forty years between them—had begun opening fire, directing their handguns toward a large banquet table in the middle of the restaurant. An old gentleman with a head more devoid of growth than the Sahara bore the brunt of their initial fire. He flung out his hands and then crashed noisily down on the table, leaking an abundance of blood. Everyone else was either diving for cover or else already there.

From behind the overturned table that he was using as his shield, Harry sighted one of the two assailants and shot him. The impact of the .44 propelled the youth back against the bamboo curtain that formed a kind of inner door. Bamboo wasn't going to stop his progress backward. His head smacked against the glass of the outer door. The glass was more resistant. It stopped the youth all right. Stopped him dead.

His companion, suddenly and uncomfortably aware that he was facing a threat from an unexpected quarter, did what amounted to a little dance, zigzagging back, transferring his fire from the banquet table to the table that Harry had converted into his temporary bastion. But because he had to do these acrobatics his aim wasn't awfully terrific. Three bullets thudded harmlessly into the waiters' station just beyond the location of Harry's table.

But because of his arduous efforts to get out of the line of fire, he was making it harder for Harry to hit him. Now he had taken refuge behind one of the several mock-Corinthian columns that distinguished the interior of the Quemoy. From there he was firing both at Harry, keeping him pinned behind the table, and at the other customers, preventing them and the waiters from moving. No one was getting hit because by this time everyone had had ample opportunity to find shelter. Harry sensed that the youth had panicked, that his only thought was to escape.

Exhausted of ammunition for the 9mm, the youth quickly substituted a snubnose .38 which he evidently carried around with him for this purpose. With no warning, he darted out from behind his protective column, driving toward the kitchen. Harry fired but knew even before he pressed the trigger that he had no chance of hitting him. The youth was moving too fast and keeping low, weaving in between the confusion of tables and chairs, firing blindly as he went along.

Abandoning the table that had defended him, Harry raced after the youth, ignoring the screams from the cowering diners who had no idea whose side Harry was on.

Approaching the kitchen, the youth blundered right into one of the cooks who'd evidently thought to take him unawares. And it was true that the youth, with his attention riveted on Harry's pursuit, failed to notice the man who barred his way right at the kitchen entrance. The cook, a short wiry man with a look of great concentration to him, was ready to bring down a heavy black pan on the youth's head. And bring it down he did with one crashing slam. It stunned the youth who reeled from the blow, but it did not succeed in knocking him out. Which was unfortunate for the cook. Turning to confront his latest assailant, the youth fired three shots at the cook, all of which entered his abdomen, with the result that his white uniform was quickly overwhelmed by blood.

But in the time that it took the youth to do this Harry had had an opportunity to gain on him. Crouching so that he could adequately target the youth, Harry fired once. His bullet slammed into the youth's neck, emerging from his throat at a sharply angled trajectory. He was dead before he fell, collapsing against the dying cook who improbably was still standing in place.

Police were pouring into the Quemoy, alerted by the sounds of gunfire and shrieking that had filtered out to the street. A horde of curious onlookers had taken up position directly outside the Quemoy, anxious not to miss any action.

The maitre d', a venerable gentleman whose memories went back to the bloody upheavals that marked the 40 Days of Peking in 1900, crawled from under the table where he'd concealed himself and regained an upright position. With as much dignity as he could summon, he stepped up to Harry and thanked him for his help. Gazing sadly at the body of the cook now collapsed on the blood-slicked kitchen floor, he said, "Without you we would have suffered a much greater loss of life."

"You know who these thugs are?"

"Not by name, no," the maitre d' said. "But we know who sent them. A gang of extortionists. They claim their actions are politically motivated, but they are simply a group of common thieves and murderers who ravage the Chinese community. It is most regrettable that they chose to make innocent people victims of their vendetta. As well as our cook. It will be difficult to find a replacement as good as him." He looked up at Harry—and Harry being as tall as he was the maitre d' had a long way to look—and with a strangely mischievous gleam in his eyes, shrugged and said, "But there is one benefit to our customers that has emerged from all this terrible violence."

"And what is that?"

"The lunches are all on the house. Especially for you, Mr. Callahan, who are such a frequent customer, you can choose whatever you'd like as an expression of our gratitude."

Harry thanked him: "But I'll have to take a rain-check. I seem to have lost my appetite."

"Would you at least care for a fortune cookie?"

"I don't think that'll be necessary. I have a good idea what kind of fortune I'm having today already."

As he strode out of the Quemoy, DiGeorgio spotted him. "What are you doing here, Harry? We send you out to Palo Alto in the morning and look where you turn up." Surveying the scene of mayhem that greeted his eyes, he muttered, "This is going to be one hell of a lot of paperwork. A field report the size of the Encyclopaedia Brittanica." He was well aware of Harry's distaste for the routine bureaucratic tasks that were necessitated by his job.

When Harry came out of the restaurant, he noticed that the tail was gone or else had found a better way to conceal himself from view. Probably shied away from this American-Chinese replay of the gunfight at the O.K. Corral, Harry considered. Well, he'd be back again. If not him then someone exactly like him.

Lunch hour was proceeding a bit more placidly at the Top of the Mark where Bull Ryan and a friend of his were leisurely working their way through a steak and lobster, supplemented by a substantial quantity of dry martinis and wine. Bull's complexion seemed to grow ruddier by the minute as his liberal imbibing continued. His friend was just about his age, but time hadn't done badly by him; his ash-gray hair only emphasized his finely etched features and his bright hazel eyes.

These two men, Bull and his dining companion, had once been irreconcilable foes, years ago during the height of labor strife on the docks. At that time the man sitting across from Bull had been a lowly patrolman whose chief occupation was to batter in the heads of union militants. But things change, and old enemies find that they have much more in common than they thought. Where there had once been bitter acrimonious disputes, there was now the sort of peaceful accord that could be honored from time to time over drinks and expensive food just as they were doing at the moment.

"I'm worried about your man Callahan," Bull was saying. "I spoke with Matt, and Matt, well, you know how he is. 'Don't concern yourself, there's no problem,' he said. But I've done a little research on Inspector Callahan. He doesn't seem to me the docile compliant type. Am I making myself clear?"

At that, Bull's friend laughed, a reaction that rather surprised Bull.

"Do you think the choice of Harry to be put on this case was accidental, my friend? You really think we'd get that careless? We're looking out for Matt's best interests, you can believe me. Harry's a man we've had our eye on for quite some time. He's a pain in the ass, quite frankly, and we've been waiting for an opportunity to—how should I put it—to get him out of the picture. This Tuber business is just perfect for our purpose."

Bull thought he understood. Callahan was being set up to take the fall. Suddenly the day seemed a whole lot brighter to him. He went back to his meal with a pleased smile on his face.

Three

Clay Meltzer was not usually the sort of man to suffer from a bad conscience. In fact, he pretty much thought that he was free of such an affliction. For a man raised on the waterfront who had willingly taken orders from a succession of petty tyrants beginning with his father, a conscience was simply a liability. But, much to his amazement, a critical juncture in his life had been reached. He was confronted with the sort of moral dilemma he never knew existed, and now he faced having to make a decision.

Meltzer occupied an insignificant role in Matt Braxton's formidable organization. He had no designated job as such; he was a gofer, a house nigger, a sometime chauffeur, sometime bodyguard. You needed coffee you sent Meltzer out to get it and then you sent him back again because he neglected to get the order right. Meltzer could just as well been a fourteen-year-old kid the way he was treated, but he was forty-nine with hair flecked with gray and a sad, lined face that had been partially dented in, mute testimony to a bloody struggle on the docks ten years before. Some people said that the blow had done something to his mental capacity. But Meltzer wasn't dumb. He just knew how to shut up and remain well in the background, obeying orders without questions, taking his salary at the end of every week and making no trouble for anybody. Which was why sometimes when serious matters arose in conversation, nobody bothered to ask Meltzer to leave. The reason was that they weren't really aware he was there to begin with.

Not that either Braxton or Bull or anyone else for that matter had actually discussed a hit on the Tubers. But the implication was clear enough to Meltzer. More obvious was the money that was passed from one hand to the other, from Braxton's man to the taciturn well-dressed fellow who had come in from Chicago; Meltzer had witnessed that, too.

But he hadn't thought about it, hadn't considered the implications of what he'd heard or seen. He kept thinking it had to do with something else, something that wasn't a hit. When enough time had elapsed and nothing had happened, he concluded that he'd been mistaken and forgot about the affair entirely.

Until yesterday morning when he'd read the papers. The fifty thousand dollar reward money meant shit, Meltzer knew. Anyone who pointed the finger at the man responsible was sure never going to collect it. That wasn't what was motivating Meltzer. And he wasn't even certain that if it had been just Bernie he'd have worried. Hell, he'd seen enough men bloodied and not a few of them killed in labor strife. He'd never cared for Bernie and his untimely departure from the world was no cause for losing any sleep. But his wife? His kids? That was what got to Meltzer, that went way beyond a vendetta.

Meltzer sat on the side of his unmade bed, smoking one cigarette after another, coughing up phlegm. He was thinking of how to go about this; he'd never had any dealings with the police before, never wanted to. He'd prefer to tip them off anonymously, but he knew that wouldn't do any good. He was a witness; his confession was the only evidence that would mean anything. He'd have to present himself in person.

Even after reaching this decision he didn't act on it right away. He walked for hours, circling around the station house, continuing the debate with himself long after he realized it was useless. At last he flung a butt into the gutter with a derisive grunt and stepped forthrightly into the San Francisco Police headquarters.

"I'm here to talk to somebody about the Tuber killing," he announced to the man at the desk.

No surprise registered on the man's face. People were constantly coming in to divulge information to the police, some of it useful, much of it specious.

"Well, you want to speak to Callahan. He's the officer on the case. But I don't think he's in right now."

Meltzer, having deliberated this long over coming here, was not about to leave without telling somebody his story. If he did leave he wasn't certain he'd get up the nerve again to come back.

"What I've got to say is important. I don't care who you get to talk to me."

"Of course, I understand. I think Officer Patel is available."

"That's fine with me. Just so long as they listen."

Officer Sandy Patel listened. He had a certain appealing boyishness to his manner—you could almost call it charm—that made him seem accessible and sympathetic. He was a fair-haired beachboy, tanned under a Malibu sun, who'd come of age. This was a man who never drank, who was working on achieving his back belt by the end of the summer, and who required just five hours of sleep to function well. He had porcelain blue eyes that invited women into his bed long before he got around to saying hello to them.

"So, Mr. Meltzer, you say you've worked for Mr. Braxton for how long?"

"For as long as he's been president. Twelve years come this October."

Meltzer was feeling rather uncomfortable; there was no ashtray anywhere to be seen and he didn't want to start flicking ashes on this police officer's floor. Recognizing his plight, Patel smiled and graciously pulled out an ashtray from a desk drawer.

"Have you made this allegation—?"

Meltzer didn't let him finish.

"Allegation! Ain't no allegation. I'm telling you the truth, what I saw with my own eyes."

"Please, it's just a habit. Legalese, you know. Let me rephrase that. Have you told anybody this story? Your wife? A friend? Anybody?"

"My wife's been dead for four years. And all my friends work for Braxton. I'd be a damn fool to tell any of them."

This somehow seemed to please Officer Patel. "Could you just wait here for a moment? There's something I have to take care of. I'll be right back."

Five minutes passed before he returned. "Thank you for waiting, Mr. Meltzer," Patel said. "You can go now. We have your phone number and when we need you we'll be in touch."

Meltzer rose from the chair, a perplexed look on his face.

"Is that all there is? Don't I see someone else?"

"Right now we're finished. Unless there's something further you wish to add?"

"No, no, I told you everything I know."

"Fine then." Patel offered his visitor one last winning smile and held open the door for him. "Have yourself a good day."

Meltzer walked slowly from the station, still bewildered. Maybe he hadn't been believed. The officer who'd seen him had hardly reacted. And he'd thought, with the kind of sensational information he had, that there'd be an uproar. But—but it was nothing.

Five minutes after Meltzer's departure Harry wandered in, looking somewhat exhausted.

"You need a vacation, Harry," one of his colleagues observed.

"Sure I need a vacation. Everybody on the planet needs a vacation."

He seated himself at his desk and began grudgingly

30

to write out his field report. He'd scarcely gotten more than a couple of lines on the page when he was interrupted by Arnold Judson, a cop who'd seen eighteen years on the force which was in his eyes about seventeen too many. It was just that he couldn't figure out what else he could be doing. "Anything happening on the Tuber case?"

Harry made the sign of a zero with his fingers.

"They tell you some guy was in here claiming he had information about it?"

"No."

"Yeah, just left a few minutes before you got here. Patel saw him."

"Patel?" Harry, always suspicious of somebody who didn't drink anything stronger than herbal teas, couldn't stand the man.

"Well, maybe I'll have a chat with Sandy Patel."

Patel was just on his way out when Harry encountered him.

"I'm told you spoke to an informant who knew something about the Tuber killing."

Patel displayed a page of typewritten notes that he held in his hand. "It's all down here, Harry. A crank if you ask me. Unreliable. I'm not sure what his angle is."

Harry glanced down at the notes. They were cursory and not at all helpful. There was only one mention of Matt Braxton buried way at the bottom of the page.

"You say here the man *used* to work for Braxton?"

"Apparently he was fired. It's possible he's out for revenge."

He looked up to find that Harry wasn't listening to him. For that matter, Harry wasn't even there.

The man at the desk in the lobby was named Emerson, no relation to Ralph Waldo.

"You sent somebody to see Patel," Harry said. "He left here maybe ten minutes ago."

"That's right."

"Describe him."

Emerson tried.

"You didn't notice which way he turned when he got out of the building?"

"Left I think it was. He was moving very slowly like he had no particular place to go."

Harry got into his car and began cruising the streets in the vicinity in hope of somehow finding Meltzer. He didn't seriously believe that he would succeed but he felt it necessary to try. That sixth sense of his was operative again, warning him that if he didn't get to Meltzer now he might never have another opportunity. Meltzer was the sort of individual other people like to turn into a statistic. But on the other hand, he was exactly the sort of individual upon whom Grand Jury indictments often hinge.

To his surprise, he observed a man who fit Meltzer's description meandering up Van Ness at a desultory pace. It was true what Emerson said; the man was certainly in no hurry. His hands were in his pocket, a cigarette was in his mouth; he looked vaguely defeated.

Harry was about a block away from him and now he proceeded to draw closer to the sidewalk and slow down. The last thing he wished to do was to frighten Clay Meltzer.

Just at that instant a olive-green Ford Galaxy in the lane parallel to Harry's accelerated, speeding ahead of Harry and cutting him off. The sound of the switching gears was deafening, like some jungle beast in its death throes.

The Galaxy pulled in toward the curb; a man on the passenger side leaned out and yelled, "Hey, Clay! How're you doing, Clay?"

Meltzer stopped in his tracks, turned to see who was addressing him.

Harry knew what was coming and he placed his foot hard down on the acclerator, gunning his car forward directly toward the Galaxy.

There wasn't any noise; the man was using a silencer and he was good at his work.

Just as Harry's car rammed right into the back of

the Galaxy, propelling it several feet up Van Ness, Meltzer slumped over and collapsed on the pavement. Pedestrians in the vicinity had no idea what was happening, unable to connect the noisy collision of the two cars with this man's keeling over. Nor did there seem to be anything obviously wrong with the man on the sidewalk at first sight. Someone was screaming, "Heart attack! The man's had a heart attack!" until Meltzer was turned over and more scrupulously examined. Then it was discovered that there were two bloody holes in his chest. Within moments he was immersed in a small but growing pool of blood as it poured out of the exit wounds in his back.

At the same time the Galaxy shot forward, pulling away from Harry's car. One glance told Harry that if Meltzer wasn't dead he was surely close to it. He directed all his attention to the pursuit of the Galaxy. The Galaxy wasn't getting very far, having a formidable amount of traffic to contend with. But that same problem made it equally difficult for Harry to maneuver. Two other cars and a Van Lines moving truck had gotten between Harry's vehicle and the one the killers were using. Some sort of tie-up seemed to have developed up ahead at the junction of Market Street. Whatever it was, neither blaring horns nor changing lights were of much help. The best you could do would be to inch forward.

Harry, cursing the downtown San Francisco traffic situation, decided that he was not about to make any progress if he remained behind the wheel. So he did the logical thing and got out of the car, abandoning it in the middle of Van Ness. A shrieking siren on Fulton Street heralded the impending arrival of an ambulance for the fallen Meltzer, but despite the crescendo of horns the ambulance wasn't getting anywhere fast either.

Darting in between the stalled cars, Harry kept low, hoping to avoid detection in the rearview mirror of the Galaxy. The other drivers, fuming at the delay, were too preoccupied to notice the man with the .44 Magnum in his hand as he made his way up to the Galaxy.

He was barely three feet away from it when abruptly

the traffic began to move. The logjam down on Market Street had apparently broken.

"Shit," Harry muttered as he watched the Galaxy beginning to pick up speed.

The driver of the car approaching Harry wasn't exactly pleased to see him blocking the way. He pounded on his horn, producing enough of a din for one of the hit men in the Galaxy to turn around. Without a moment's hesitation, Harry fired, first at the Galaxy's rear window, turning much of its glass to a fine dust and creating a spiderweb of lines through what remained of it. With the explosion of glass it was impossible to see whether he'd succeeded in hitting anyone. Now he fired at the rear tires, puncturing them so that they began immediately to deflate. The incapacitated Galaxy screeched as the driver fought to navigate it out of the line of fire. And in spite of its crippled back wheels the car was still moving forward though on an erratic course. Again Harry fired, mindless of the confusion of traffic that surrounded him, but this time managed only to strike the chrome bumper; the bullet ricocheted with a lot of noisy metallic clanking.

Whether by intention or because the driver had lost control of his car, the Galaxy swerved abruptly and collided with a pickup truck in the next lane. Fenders crumpled like paper but the Galaxy still kept going. But it had become locked to the pickup truck and was dragging it along, much to the outrage of the truck's driver who was clinging to the wheel, forlornly trying to extricate his vehicle.

Harry was tearing after the Galaxy and its unwanted mate, no longer firing because it was senseless to do so until he came within range. And having no time to reload, he did not wish to squander what remained of his ammunition, since it was abundantly clear he would have to save some for the occupants of the wounded Galaxy.

But as he made his approach, coming up within five yards of his target, which was about to bound over a curb and knock over a hydrant, still dragging along the pickup truck, a shot struck a parking meter directly to Harry's

34

right. Turning, Harry looked to see where the shot had come from and in doing so just avoided a second one. Both were obviously meant for him.

He quickly threw himself down on the pavement and crawled behind a parked car. Two additional shots came from out of nowhere; whoever was shooting at him was not all that interested in hurting him; rather his objective was to keep Harry pinned down. And in that he was being very successful.

All at once there was a resounding crash that might have signaled the apocalypse or at least the dress rehearsal for it. But from his vantage point Harry couldn't see what precisely had caused it—the Galaxy, the pickup truck, or some other moving or unmoving object that had gotten in their way. The air was filled with the raucous staccato sounds of sirens from every point of the compass. Well, Harry considered, if I don't get those sons of bitches someone else will.

No additional shots were coming at him and so Harry rose, testing the altitude. It seemed safe enough. Seeing Harry, others did likewise, crawling out from temporary shelters.

Around the corner a crowd had gathered to look at the Ford Galaxy's burial ground which was a drugstore. The car had swept right into the plate glass window and crashed inside, doing as much damage to the interior, with its racks of pharmaceutical supplies, as it did to the druggist and one of the customers, both of whom lay dead under the ruptured tires. Another customer, his head washed over with blood from a deep scalp wound, looked to Harry like he could make instant use of the entire collection of drugs still left intact scattered through the store.

The pickup truck had come to a rest not far away though still in the street. It was upside down. The driver, shouting in fury, was crawling out of the vehicle, evidently none the worse for his experience.

But where the hit men had gone, Harry was at a loss to say. One man allowed that he had seen them scamper away while the car was still moving, throwing open the doors and bolting. He said there were three men, another man claimed two. But two or three, they had, with the aid of their unseen ally who'd pinned Harry down, achieved their escape.

And Harry had a feeling he knew who this ally was— the same man who'd tailed him around the city in the morning and stood watch outside the Quemoy Inn.

There'd be statements taken from witnesses, of course, and the Galaxy's license and registration would be checked out. The police might even decide to cordon off the area for a couple of hours while they searched for Meltzer's killers, but Harry knew, with that sixth sense of his, that none of these stratagems would do any good. When you dealt with professionals like this you worked against the odds.

Thinking back on the incident, he recalled how Sandy Patel had dismissed Meltzer as a crank, a disaffected out-of-work flunky who was anxious to spread malicious rumors about Braxton. No one usually put a contract out on a poor bastard like that unless someone took him seriously. Very seriously.

Patel bears watching, Harry thought. Can't prove shit now maybe, but he bears watching. Problem is who else in the department also bears watching and how far up you have to look.

Four

The woman in the double bed moved languorously; the sun, ruthlessly exposed as soon as the curtains were drawn, struck her face with such insistence that it succeeded in pulling her up from a sustained sleep. Groaning at the unwelcome onset of consciousness, she threw a sheet up over her head, leaving only an unruly trickle of honey-blonde hair in view.

"Come on, Darlene, rise and shine. It's nearly noon. You don't want to miss the day."

Seeing that Darlene had no intention of complying, Matt Braxton, already shaven and dressed to the nines in a black tux, strode over to the bed and gripping hold of the top of the pink silk sheet, tugged it down, flinging it off the bed entirely so that she could not easily retrieve it.

What Braxton liked about Darlene was that she looked practically as good in daylight, with the sun full on her, as she did at night. What he didn't like about her was most everything else: her personality, her flamboyance, her tendency to gossip incessantly. Why he kept coming back to her he couldn't begin to imagine.

Well that wasn't exactly true. That body, lithe but with just enough flesh to hold onto, no *Vogue*-like emaciation, full breasts, fuller ass, that body was why he kept coming back. And that face, always saying: I want, I want, I want, but always implying: You're the only one who can give it to me the way I like. That face, too, kept him coming back. It was like a goddamn addiction.

Worse than the compulsion were the doubts Darlene constantly aroused in him; he was sure she was screwing around on the side, that any number of men in his organization had balled her at one time or another, but the bitch of it was he couldn't prove a thing. The detectives he hired to spy on her could come up with only the most fragile evidence of any infidelity. He had the feeling that she knew when he suspected her and made certain that her behavior was irreproachable at those times. Braxton's temper she knew was a thing to be feared.

But even threats, veiled or explicit, were not enough to assure Braxton of her loyalty. He lavished her with jewelry and clothes—designer wear purchased at exorbitant Beverly Hills boutiques. He gave her a cream-color Cadillac Seville and a chauffeur to drive her around in it. But how could he stop her from admiring young men or at least from thinking of them and the day she would be free of Matt Braxton?

She was twenty-eight, Braxton was more than thirty years beyond that. Not that he was in bad condition for someone his age; the formidable muscular frame of his body, built up after years of labor on the docks, had suffered only minor erosion. Matt Braxton was a man on the move, no sedentary existence for him. Arthritic aches, neuralgic irritation he ignored. If he went out, he wanted it to be all at once—light, then darkness—no gradual withering away of the body and spirit by illness and senility.

But he did not contemplate departing this earth any time soon. On the contrary, he was convinced that he was going to be around for many years to come. And so long as he was around, he wanted Darlene to be around for him—when it was convenient.

"Darlene, get up, I'm telling you for the last time."

Darlene, still refusing to open her eyes, protested. "Why should I have to get up? You're the one who has to go somewhere. I don't."

"I don't have to explain to you."

He threw her bathrobe at her. It landed across her belly.

"Come here, Matt, love, come here."

He stepped closer to the bed. Eyes popping open, she sat up, snaring Braxton with her arms. She attempted to pull him down on the bed with her.

"I don't have time for this. Don't mess my jacket, would you?"

Extricating himself from her embrace, he strode from the room, slamming the door definitively behind him. Not that he was angry or even annoyed. He just liked to slam doors.

Grumbling still, Darlene addressed her absent lover.

"All right, my lord and master, you son of a bitch, I'm getting up."

Although no formal announcement had been made, the members of the press who turned out to cover the luncheon in honor of retiring Senator Camden Halloway were not expecting either Matt Braxton or John Bull Ryan to show up. After all, only three days had passed since the Tuber slayings and people generally assumed that the Brotherhood leaders would stay away out of deference to the deceased.

This did not turn out to be the case. Bull arrived first, accompanied by a retinue of advisers and bodyguards, distinguishable by the dark glasses that kept their eyes from view.

Bull had earlier leaked rumors to the press asserting that he, too, might be a target of some dark conspiracy directed at the union itself.

But it was not Bull who elicited the most attention but Braxton, whose creased weather-beaten face seemed to reflect concern and solemnity in keeping with his public condemnation of the dissident union activist's death. No sooner had he stepped into the lobby of the Fairmont than photographers and TV cameramen clustered around him, showering him with brilliant light. Try as he might, Braxton could not resist smiling for all of them. It was too much of a habit for him to give up all at once. However, when he was asked for a statement he refused to give out one. "We are here today to honor our great senator, Camden Halloway. I don't want to spoil this occasion by discussing the sad events of recent days. Thank you, gentlemen." There were women present among the press corps, but Braxton did not acknowledge them, might not even have noticed them.

Like Bull, Braxton was accompanied by a small army of cohorts; telltale bulges in their jackets afforded ample evidence that they were all armed.

The luncheon was a huge success; the roast beef was tasty and had not turned lukewarm during its long journey from the kitchen, the drinks were strong and plentiful, the conversation affable and sporadically informative, the mood festive, more so because of the brevity of the speeches.

Braxton uncharacteristically rejected all efforts to get him to speak, averring that it was John Bull Ryan who was president of the Brotherhood and who should therefore be the one to deliver the necessary laudatory remarks. An aide to Braxton whispered in his ear that Bull was not yet president since the union elections had been postponed. This reminder drew an uproarious laugh from Braxton. "Oh?" he asked the aide, "do you know anyone who's going to oppose him?"

So Bull gave the encomium, reading from the speech prepared for him and given him only a few minutes ago. Not having bothered to read the speech before, his delivery was halting. No one minded. After all, no one was really listening.

In conclusion, Bull warmly praised the senator, who beamed proudly from the dias, and expressed his union's gratitude for all the political favors Camden Halloway had done for it while in Washington. At the same time he hoped that Halloway's successor, Senator Lex Lewis, would keep in mind the union's needs in the future. From the benign expression on Lex Lewis' face, you sensed that the Brotherhood was already on his mind; he didn't need to get to Capitol Hill to start becoming aware of its power.

Close to three in the afternoon the sated diners emerged from the banquet hall, drifting out through the lobby. The press had already gone home. There were no flashbulbs popping in the faces of the dignitaries and the honored guests. As a result, the security was not quite so rigorous; the men surrounding Matt Braxton didn't quite box him in the way they had when he'd entered the lobby at noon. In any case, Braxton wouldn't let them; there were friends to chat with and he didn't like having body-guards looming over his shoulders. Braxton did not think he feared death.

As he was engaging in conversation with Frank Telso, Halloway's press secretary, he suddenly realized that another party, an uninvited party, had decided to join in on the discussion.

Braxton studied the intruder not with anger so much as with surprise.

"Excuse me, sir, but if you don't mind I am talking to this gentleman."

The offending presence refused to move. Instead he drew from his pocket his wallet and opened it up to display a badge.

"Inspector Harry Callahan," Braxton said. "Why does that name sound familiar?"

"I'd like to speak to you a minute," Harry said politely as possible.

"In regard to what?"

"The death of Bernard Tuber."

"I've told the police what I know. But if you'd like, you can make an appointment with my secretary. I'll be happy to talk to you next week. I am always delighted to cooperate with the police."

"I'm afraid your secretary hasn't been very helpful."

41

Braxton exchanged a knowing look with Telso.

"Well, let me speak to her. I guarantee you an appointment. Early next week, what do you say to that?"

Braxton obviously did not expect Harry to object. Braxton wasn't a man accustomed to opposition.

"I have this problem," said Harry. "I don't like waiting."

Braxton shrugged, still maintaining his composure, his smile seemingly permanently affixed to his lips.

"That's unfortunate, *Mr.* Callahan. I don't especially like waiting either. Now if you'll excuse me I have to be on my way. I am a very busy man."

"That may very well be, but I am going to have to delay you."

Braxton's face became flushed. Annoyance was turning into anger. He was about to reprove Harry, but decided that the detective was only bluffing. Instead of arguing further, he started to move away from Harry. Meanwhile, a number of his aides and bodyguards milling in the vicinity, their attention drawn to the stranger confronting their boss, stepped in close to Braxton, pretty much surrounding Harry.

Undeterred by their presence, Harry simply shifted to the right, effectively blocking Braxton's passage.

"I am not about to ask you again, Callahan, would you please get out of my way? I am not used to being abused in this way." Braxton looked pointedly at his security people and then back to Harry in tacit warning.

The prospect of an imminent confrontation was observed by several people in the lobby. Curious, they, too, began to gravitate toward Braxton and Harry.

With more and more onlookers congregating about, Braxton only felt more confident. He doubted that this one detective would attempt anything provocative under so much public scrutiny. So once again he began to move around Harry. And once again Harry refused to let him pass.

Without waiting for a word or a signal from Braxton, one of the bodyguards reached forward, gripping Harry's right arm decisively to pull him back. Without hesitation, Harry swung his free arm around, slapping the side of his hand against the bodyguard's neck while simultaneously stabbing him in the ribs with his right elbow. The bodyguard, astonished, found himself suddenly off-balance. He stumbled and fell and in doing so, nearly knocked Braxton off his feet as well.

Another bodyguard was about to attack Harry when Braxton held up his hand to stop him. While the groaning man at his feet slowly picked himself up off the floor, Braxton addressed Harry. The smile was back on his face. "You are a most determined man, Callahan. If you're so anxious to ask me whatever questions you have on your mind, ask away. I'm at your disposal."

"I'd prefer a little more privacy. Send your clowns back to the circus."

Braxton chose to overlook the insult. The fact was that he didn't think much of the men who guarded him either. He nodded at his men, and they quietly withdrew, taking up positions several yards away, like a battalion digging in.

"So what do you want to know?" Braxton asked, feigning a convivial attitude.

Harry knew that Braxton, failing to humiliate him by ignoring him, had switched to another tack. He was now trying to humor him. It was all Harry could do to restrain himself.

"How long has it been since you fired Clay Meltzer?"

"I didn't fire—" Braxton began, then stopped himself. "What's this about Clay? I thought you wanted to talk about Tuber."

"I do. I am. I think you're aware they're related, Mr. Braxton. What did Clay Meltzer do for you?"

"I don't know. Meltzer was one of Bull's boys. I hardly knew the man."

"Why do you think he was murdered?"

"Frankly, I have no idea. I know only what I read in

43

the papers. I suppose it was some private dispute. Some members of our union, as I'm sure you know, well, they get drunk, pick a fight—" His voice trailed off.

"You couldn't have been reading too carefully. Clay Meltzer was killed by a gunman while he was walking down the street."

"It's unfortunate, regrettable."

"I assume then that you wouldn't mind me looking at the files your organization has on Meltzer."

"That will probably require a court order. But I'm not at liberty to say. After all, I'm no longer in charge of the day-to-day affairs of the Brotherhood. For that sort of information you're going to have to speak to Bull."

"If he's the best ventriloquist you can come up with," Harry said, walking away, "then you got problems."

Braxton wasn't certain that he had triumphed in this confrontation. Actually he felt that somehow he had given out information that he shouldn't have had. And why was Callahan concentrating so much on Meltzer? Meltzer was nothing. Nothing in life, nothing in death. Matt Braxton wasn't about to see the empire he had so arduously constructed over so many years collapse merely because of a fuckup like Clay Meltzer and a prying cop named Harry Callahan.

"It was nothing," Braxton told his aides as he rejoined them. "The cop's on a fishing expedition is all."

Within minutes Braxton had virtually forgotten about Harry. He and his companions piled into the awaiting limousines whose windows were blackened so that no one could peer in. But you could see out of them with no problem.

Braxton's limo was partway down Mason when one of the bodyguards with a sharper eye than most happened to notice that they were being followed.

"Who is it?" Braxton asked, his buoyant mood in danger of being shaken yet again.

"The cop. The goddamn cop. He's making no effort to cover himself. He wants us to know he's there."

44

"I have a feeling that this bastard's going to get on my nerves and soon."

The last people to have gotten on Braxton's nerves had had cause to regret it.

Five

Harry was a desperate man. Basically, in the Tuber case he had nothing, not a shred of evidence that would tie any suspect in with the killings, let alone Braxton or any members of his union. There was nothing new from Redhorn or the Palo Alto police. Nor were any of the leads provided by Redhorn's favorite computer system—PATRIC—proving to be of help.

About the only strategy that he had adopted was to hang close to Braxton. Close, admittedly, wasn't close enough. He could seldom even get to see the man. His car, yes, his bodyguards and aides, yes, but Braxton himself just twice from across the street; Braxton lived and moved in such splendid isolation that Harry began wondering whether he didn't have somebody who ate his food for him to save him the trouble.

Harry knew that Braxton was behind Tuber's death and behind Meltzer's, and yet he could not justify his persistent surveillance to Bressler.

"You tell me you're operating on a hunch," Bressler said, never once looking Harry directly in the eyes.

They were in Bressler's office. Tuber and his wife and children had been dead for a week and a half. That was six days away from being front-page news and three days away from being news at all. All anyone talked about was the Giants' chances to win the pennant. It was too hot, too much August, to pay attention to anything

46

else. Murder and corruption in high places could wait until fall.

"That's correct. I would stake my life on it."

"It might not be your life, Harry. It may be just a little thing like your career. I know in the past you've seemed uncommonly anxious to throw away your career. If you feel that way now, Harry, why don't you let me know now, save us both the trouble."

Harry was silent.

"Because I'll tell you one thing. I've gotten complaints about your behavior in the last couple of days."

Harry knew what was coming but thought he'd ask anyway. "Oh? What sort of complaints, Lieutenant?"

"You are accused of harassing a citizen for no other purpose than to intimidate him. You know who I'm talking about."

"What is this harassment supposed to consist of, mind my asking?"

"Come off it, Harry." Bressler was losing his patience. "Do I have to spell everything out for you? No one gave you any directive to follow Matt Braxton around town. No one told you to watch his every movement, to station yourself outside his home. If that's what I want you to do, I'll tell you."

"What happened to personal initiative?"

"Personal initiative, my ass. With you, personal initiative means blowing someone away with that cannon of yours. The only reason you're still with this department is because you've been lucky. Luck doesn't last forever. That's what they call the law of probability, Harry. Now get out of my office. And if I hear that you're still shopping Braxton, I'm taking you off the case. Understand me?"

"Every word, Lieutenant."

Harry left the office but what was on his mind wasn't the upbraiding he'd just been subjected to; that had been anticipated. What truly interested him was just who had sent the word to Bressler to lay off of Braxton. He doubted it had come from Braxton directly. Braxton wasn't the sort of man to deal with a mere homicide lieutenant. He had gone to someone higher up. But whom? For the first time he began to feel that maybe it didn't make much sense to tail Braxton around Nob Hill and the Embarcadero. Could be he was following the wrong person.

There was a bar a block or so away from the station house. Safest goddamn bar in town since it was frequented mostly by cops who, whether they were in or out of uniform, were always packing pieces on them. A would-be stickup man would have to be a suicidal lunatic to attempt to rip off the joint.

It was approaching in on eveningtime; the bar was filling up with men just coming off their shifts, desperate for the invigoration a couple of cold brews could provide. Outside the air had stopped moving; with no place special to go, it sat there in the bay, stuperously hot, waiting for a fog or a fresh breeze from the Pacific to dispel it.

Arnold Judson wandered in and took a stool next to Harry.

"How're you doing, Harry?"

"I have no idea, Arnie. None at all."

"You were in with Bressler."

"Word gets around, doesn't it?"

Judson ordered a double shot of Red Label and a beer back. He then turned to Harry. "This Tuber shit's eating you up. You getting any sleep? Don't answer that. You know what I think?"

"I don't want to know what you think." Harry stared morosely at his reflection in the mirror behind the bar. He wasn't particularly happy with what he saw.

"I don't care whether you want to know what I think because I'm going to tell you. I'm telling you that you ain't getting any sleep. You look like shit. You're busting your ass over this one and why? I know why. You bust your ass over every case. OK, I think that's really fine. Rare in this day and age, but I'm all for it. But you fucking damn well know that all you're going to come up against is a goddamn stone wall. Everybody knows Braxton had Tuber hit. But no one wants to prove it. And you know why they don't?"

"I don't want to know," Harry said, realizing that it made no difference to Judson.

"I'll tell you why. Because if anything happens to Braxton there's going to be a wildcat strike on the docks. And the city is in no mood to stand for a strike. It means too much to the economy, and you don't need to be told how shitty the city's economy is these days. Just look at your goddamn paycheck. When was the last time we got a raise that could buy you more than another beer every week? So, as one cop to the other, let me tell you, Harry, the best thing you can do is forget it."

"Forget it?"

"Hey, no, I don't mean forget it. I mean, well, hell, I don't know what I mean. I mean you don't have to eat, sleep, and drink this case."

Harry glanced down at the whiskey in front of him. "Well, I don't know about that last part."

Just as he spoke, Judson directed Harry's attention down to the other end of the bar. "Talk about drinking, here comes the force's representative of the Women's Christian Temperance Union."

Harry looked to where Judson was pointing. Sandy Patel had just come in. He was in his uniform; it looked as crisp and ungodly fresh as he did.

"What'd he do, renounce abstinence? I've never seen him here before."

"No, no, nothing like that. Patel get pissed? Never happen. He orders orange juice, Perrier, some shit like that. You watch."

Just as Judson predicted, Patel asked for a large glass of orange juice which he hastily downed, then hurried out.

"The pause that refreshes," Judson mumbled.

"Maybe I have been following the wrong person," said Harry, abruptly abandoning his seat.

"What did you say, Harry? Hey, where are you going?"

Patel was alone in his squad car, one of the few members of the department who'd volunteered to ride solo. The object was to spread the police around, give them a greater presence. But there was a serious drawback, as far as the Benevolent Association saw it, and that was that a patrol officer couldn't rely on the immediate backup a partner would provide.

But Patel claimed he preferred the solitude and didn't mind going it alone, and as far as his colleagues were concerned that was fine with them. A guy like Patel, who doesn't smoke, doesn't drink, hardly ever swears, keeps to himself, never accepts invitations out when he's off-duty, doesn't exactly endear himself to the people he works with.

It struck Harry though, as he tailed the unsuspecting patrolman through the North Beach sector, that there might be another motive Patel had for keeping his own company, something besides an obsession with privacy (Harry knew about that, suffered it too often), something behind the smug attitude he manifested, the I-can-handle-any-shit-they-throw-at-me attitude. Riding solo gave him the opportunity to move freely. You report in but there's no one by your side to maintain tabs on you; no one you have to cut in on a deal so that he won't turn you in out of frustrated greed, no one to suspect you of anything at all.

The intersection of Broadway and Columbus was ablaze with lights, primary colors blinking on and off with mesmerizing rhythms, advertising the delights of the flesh to the accompaniment of loud brassy music, Donna Summer and Gloria Gaynor blasting out of every other hole in the wall. Lean, aggressive men half-hidden in the shadows were calling out to the passersby: "Girls, girls, girls, check 'em out, don't cost you nothin' to look!"

Patel was stopping a block beyond this famous intersection, double-parking, leaving the motor running. He disappeared into the door of a topless joint that once used to be a decent jazz club. Not that Harry minded the topless joint; it was just that the dancers there were so damn ugly that you knew something else was going on. No way a place like that could pull in the rent each month with those girls alone.

Patel was back in five minutes. He thrust something into his pocket and looked around, possibly expecting to see somebody he knew. Then he returned to his car and pulled away, continuing down Broadway.

Harry was listening in on the police band; he was hearing exactly what Patel was hearing.

But it was only when the dispatcher addressed Patel directly that he sat up and took notice.

"Car 42 . . . Car 42 . . ."

Patel picked up. "This is Car 42."

"We have a report of an eleven-two in progress at the corner of Fifth and Mission. Two men both armed."

"Ten-four."

Patel's squad car made its existence known with a wailing siren as he continued along Columbus. Harry followed him into Montgomery and then onto Market and down Fifth.

At first it was impossible to determine what was happening at the corner. Patel, a 9mm high-powered Browning gripped steadily in his hand, got out of his car and began walking toward the corner. A man dashed up to him and grabbed him on the arm so suddenly that Patel seemed ready to blow him away.

"Not there, Officer," the man cried. "Down to your right. That pawnshop. A spade and a white dude."

Patel turned and raced toward where the man had pointed. Harry by this time had parked his own car and was just half a block behind Patel. Much as he disliked Patel, Harry was prepared to back him up; he wasn't about to let even a corrupt and arrogant cop get killed by low-lifes on the street if he could help it.

A faint light shone through the rectangular window of the pawn shop, which was cluttered with clock radios, Motorolas, Sony color TVs, an electric typewriter, and a harpsicord, of all things. The iron grill fence that ordinarily protected the shop at night had been pulled halfway to the door. Maybe the pawnbroker had forgotten something while closing up and gone back inside. Maybe he was interrupted and forced back.

In any case, you couldn't really see anything. The interior was mostly bathed in darkness. The pawnbroker must have relied on a silent alarm under the counter, Harry thought.

Patel, still unaware of Harry's presence in the vicinity, moved cautiously into the doorway, flattening himself out against the narrow wall so as to avoid being spotted from within. Then, slowly, he took hold of the door knob and twisted it to the right. Nothing happened. It was locked.

So Patel shot out the lock, kicked the door halfway open, and went down into a crouch.

Reaction to this was practically instantaneous—not on the part of the two would-be robbers but from the store's owner. The problem was that the robbers, still with their handguns directed on the pawnbroker, hadn't yet mobilized themselves to deal with this latest threat. The pawnbroker, a corpulent figure who looked like he suffered from a terrible disposition, was certain that Patel's invasion had given him the opportunity he was waiting for.

Reaching below the counter he came up with a gun of his own.

"Freeze! Freeze, you're under arrest!" Patel was shouting.

Harry was a couple of feet away from him, but stayed well to his right, not wanting to endure the barrage of bullets should the men fail to obey Patel's instruction.

And in fact, the two men would have frozen were it not for the pawnbroker who seemed reluctant to be deprived of his moment of glory. Evidently unappreciative of Patel's rescue effort, he trained his gun on the white member of the pair and discharged it. They were so close to each other that only a blind man could have missed.

The white, a bearded mother of around forty, staggered with the impact, but he wasn't quite ready to lay down and die. He fired back, now at the pawnbroker, now at Patel. It was a Luger he had and while it was only firing .22s, it was making a huge racket. Patel had ducked back, out of the line of fire, shooting back but not with any great effect since he was unable to see around the corner and into the pawnshop.

The pawnbroker, having the ill fortune not to have ducked in time himself, looked vastly surprised by the way everything had developed. How many times he'd been punctured by .22s was impossible to determine, but a ship could have set sail on the blood that rushed out over his clothes. He refused, however, to acknowledge defeat. He raised his gun with difficulty and was about to shoot again when a 9mm bullet pierced his head. He had gotten in the way of Patel's fire. Harry was the only one to realize this but he was in no position to do anything about it—and come to think about it what could he do?—being forced to lay low while the wounded white partner in this misconceived operation continued to spray the street with a hail of bullets.

What the .22s couldn't do the 9mm cartridge surely did. The pawnbroker, astonished that life should terminate so abruptly and on this particular August night, lurched over and collapsed with a final groan.

The white, himself critically wounded, was no longer in command of his faculties. His shooting was dangerous and erratic; he seemed to have no special target in mind. Blood, in systolic rhythm, spurted out from a wound at the base of his neck. And when he opened his mouth, almost as if to say something, blood crested up from his throat and dribbled down his chin.

His tall black companion looked simply appalled at the way things were working out. Whatever the plans he and his dying partner had contrived, obviously didn't include this kind of shit. He was, just like Patel and Harry, ducking, crawling along the floor, doing his utmost to save his ass, swearing up and down that should he emerge whole from this melee he would be happy to serve God, country, and the Man, in whichever order was necessary. "God help me!" he kept screaming. "Somebody help me! Don't have to be God!"

Patel risked stretching his head out into the doorway to see if he could capture a better glimpse of the madman who refused to be shut down. He nearly got his scalp singed by a passing bullet for his trouble. Like a turtle disappointed with what it sees, he retracted his head immediately.

Harry crept way around, crossing Fifth, taking no notice of the terrified pedestrians who, having scattered at the sound of the first shot, were now peering out from doorways and windows.

It was clear that the white had another weapon, maybe a couple more to supplement the Luger. No way of telling. But he kept on firing. Weak as he was, he wouldn't stop shooting. And with the pawnbroker out of the running, he had apparently settled on taking random potshots at the street.

Harry, taking refuge behind a parked car, rose above the hood just enough to get the crazed dying bastard in sight. Carefully aiming his .44, he fired.

The white man gave out a shriek that might have awakened the dead he was shortly to have as company, then he seemed to levitate for a moment before collapsing backward, thrown by the force of the bullet that had entered his belly and sprung out in back, taking sizable chunks of vital organs in its passage.

"Oh shit, oh fuck! This is some crazy shit!" the black was muttering, his hands over his head in a supplicant gesture, his gun tossed aside.

Patel meanwhile was having a hard time understanding what had happened, why this intense little engagement he'd had going had come to such an abrupt end.

He was unable to see Harry because Harry had gone down behind the car, uncertain that the danger was over. Nor with the darkness in the shop could he see that the dead man's partner was ready to surrender.

When it was evident that the firing had ceased,

Harry stood up again, but by that time Patel had gone charging into the pawnshop, his 9mm Browning ready to speed whomever had survived into the next world.

Harry, convinced neither of Patel's competence nor of his sense of mercy, hastened across the street, right behind him.

Patel was under the impression no one was watching him; he figured he had a few moments to earn a medal without a witness to say that maybe he didn't deserve it. If he wondered about who had fired the bullet that took the white out he didn't seem to let it stop him from putting his gun to the survivor's head.

He wanted to kill him, to prove he had achieved some kind of victory here, little realizing that it was his gun that had succeeded in killing the man he was supposed to be protecting. True, he hadn't intended to but it would be a bit of an embarrassment for him.

"Oh man, don't! Oh shit, man, please! My gun ain't even loaded. Check it out."

Patel had his finger on the trigger, in no mood for such excuses.

Harry was sure Patel would have fired if he hadn't interrupted.

"Party's over, Sandy."

Patel glanced up; irritation showed in his face but he left it out of his voice.

"I should have guessed. You were the one who got him then?" He gestured towards the fallen man whose body was still pumping out blood, trying to get rid of it all before the embalmer had to do it instead.

"That's right."

"You shouldn't have done that, Harry. It was my show. I could have handled it. You're not absolutely indispensible."

He was still looming over the black man, the Browning poised at the man's temple.

"I'm awfully sorry about that, Sandy, but if I hadn't interrupted, this shooting match might have gone on forever." Sandy scowled and made some unfortunate remark under his breath. Harry ignored him. "Besides, I was rather worried you might hit another innocent bystander." Noticing Patel's look of incomprehension, he gestured to the fallen pawnbroker. "The .22s didn't bring him down, it was your Browning that did it. Don't believe me? Wait until ballistics checks on that wound in the head."

Obviously Patel didn't believe him; he sensed that Harry was playing some sort of a trick on him for motives he couldn't immediately discern. In any case, he still had his gun on the man lying prostrate on the floor.

"I think you can safely let the suspect stand up."

Sandy didn't care to do this, evidently not having abandoned his notion of blowing someone away—intentionally this time.

"How many times you got to be told, Sandy?"

Patel, flushing with anger, raised his gun.

Gratefully, the black dared to look up. For the first time, his eyes met Harry's. There was immediate recognition.

"Officer Callahan!"

"Well, I'll be damned. Longlegs!"

Patel's face was filled with his perplexity and annoyance. He might have suspected that the two were confederates.

Well, they weren't confederates exactly, but they were old acquaintances you could say. Longlegs was a man with a rap sheet that could compete favorably in length with *War and Peace*. The guy had done time for cashing fraudulent checks, thieving cars, pickpocketing, sticking up five & dimes, grocery stores, gas stations, and greasy spoons; he'd been served summons for loitering, for drunk and disorderly conduct, for peddling hot watches, for creating a disturbance with a mother of a transistor radio; beyond that, he was suspected of contributing to a variety of scams, con jobs, felonies, and misdemeanors. He couldn't help it. It was in his nature. He didn't mean any harm by what he did nor did he ever hurt anyone— their pocketbooks maybe but not their bodies. So it did

56

not surprise Harry when he picked up Longlegs' gun and found that it was not loaded.

Longlegs was maybe in his forties. He was in any case one of those whose age remains a perpetual enigma; truly he had a lean and hungry face with sad, slitted brown eyes and a mouth that seemed to droop in a state of permanent melancholia. You could tell he never expected anything to go right, was just going through the motions in desperate hope of beating the odds. He'd gained his nickname—his real name was long ago buried beneath a barrage of aliases, so many that even he'd probably forgotten the one he'd started out with—not because his legs were particularly long but rather because he'd once entertained tourists down on Fisherman's Wharf by parading about on stilts.

Right now Longlegs needed more than stilts to get around. Police sirens, ambulance sirens were shrieking up and down Mission.

Harry turned to Patel. "I'm taking Longlegs into custody myself."

Patel didn't like this idea. Without Longlegs he was left with two dead bodies. Dead bodies aren't particularly articulate when it comes to clarifying how they had arrived in their current condition.

"He's mine."

"Not any more."

Longlegs looked dazedly from one man to the other. "What is this shit? I'm supposed to go to the highest bidder?"

"You're coming with me, Longlegs."

Longlegs didn't seem willing to move without a guarantee that rising to a vertical position wouldn't jeopardize his health. But Harry was impatient, and he decided he'd better risk it.

"Where are you taking him, Harry?"

"That's my business. Your business is to explain how a 9mm cartridge got into that guy's skull there. Maybe you could tell our friends on the force about Clay

57

Meltzer's unemployment status. But I suppose you're saving that for later, aren't you, Sandy?"

"Son of a bitch," was Patel's succinct commentary.

Just as Harry and his charge began to emerge from the battle site, they were confronted by DiGeorgio and three officers Harry vaguely recognized.

"What is this, Harry? Every goddamn disaster and you're there! You addicted to trouble?"

"That's right."

DiGeorgio's eyes moved to the right into the pawnshop. The extent of the carnage appeared to be greater at first glance than it actually was, with all the wreckage and the blood.

"What happened here?"

"Sandy'll explain. It's his show."

"Patel?" DiGeorgio grunted. He felt about the man more or less as Harry did. Now he seemed to notice Longlegs. In his eyes lay an unspoken question: What the hell does he have to do with this?

"Longlegs, you know DiGeorgio?"

Longlegs was like an actor who, without the benefit of either a script or a rehearsal, found himself thrust out on center stage with no choice but to perform—or do something.

"No, sir, don't believe we have met."

His manner was so polite and deferential that DiGeorgio was instantly suspicious.

"I busted him on Sixth for lifting a wallet from some poor sucker. Then I heard the shooting and came down to see what the fun was. I brought along Longlegs, figured he'd get a kick out of it."

DiGeorgio had better things to do than to puzzle out Harry's remarks.

"I want to know one thing, Harry."

"Yeah, what's that?"

"When are you going to say one blessed thing I can believe?"

"That time hasn't come yet." He turned to Longlegs. "We got to get your ass down to the station, my friend."

To Longlegs anything was possible tonight. But of one thing he was certain; for whatever inscrutable reasons Harry had, he wasn't going to be tied in with what had gone on in the pawnship. And that made Longlegs an extremely happy man.

Harry motioned Longlegs into his car. He didn't say a word to him until he'd driven down to a location on the Embarcadero on the edge of the bay. It was dark and there was no one around. Which was exactly how Harry wanted it.

Longlegs was growing uneasy. Having anticipated a ride to the station house, a ride he was by now very familiar with, he was mystified to find himself in this desolate part of the city. His relief at having escaped blame for the pawnshop mess was turning into apprehension.

Although Harry had stopped the car he left the motor running. A sign he meant to be brief.

"Longlegs, let me know if I'm wrong. But my impression is that you know a shitload of people on the streets."

Longlegs knew Harry was getting at something but what? That he couldn't figure out.

"Oh yeah, I know lots of people. What kind of people you got in mind, officer Callahan?"

"Scumbags generally. Professional scumbags."

Longlegs caught a glimmer of what Harry was driving at but only a glimmer. "Maybe I'm dense but—?"

"Hit men, Longlegs. People who command a great deal of cash for their services. People who know how to avoid heat."

"Hey, Harry, you got me wrong. What happened tonight that was Lee's fault. I didn't even know his fuckin' piece was loaded, man. We were going in there to scare the dude. I didn't think Lee would pull that shit. I swear I don't know what got into him."

Harry wasn't remotely interested in his protests or apologies.

"Longlegs, my man, you do not seem to understand.

59

I do not care about tonight. I do not care about your late friend Lee. I am more interested in the connections you enjoy right now. On the streets of our good city. You are going to find me some men whose business it is to dispatch other people to the next world."

"Harry? Oh, come on, where am I supposed to find dudes like that? I'm a small-time man. What do I know? I'm simply chomp change. You need somebody else, not me."

"No, there you're wrong, Longlegs. As of now you are working for me. Think of it as a temporary assignment. You find these people, you find them and you tell them you been hearing about some fellow, man with lots of bucks interested in arranging a hit. Give them the name Mark Kincaid. From now on in it's Mark Kincaid when you refer to me. Understand?"

Longlegs' eyes widened with fear. "Shit, you got to be crazy, man. I mean you just got to be one crazy motherfucker."

"That may be, that very well may be. You think about it. Consider the alternative."

There wasn't much to consider. With his record, Longlegs could look forward to celebrating a good many birthdays behind bars.

"You're asking an awful lot."

"Goodnight, Longlegs."

Longlegs was about to get out of the car, but he still had one further question for Harry. "Supposin' I should just split town, I could to that and you'd be out one well-connected spade."

Harry laughed. "You could make it from here to Tierra del Fuego and you know I'd find you."

Longlegs rolled his head back and laughed, too. "The Man got you, he got you," Longlegs said, and those were his parting words.

Harry watched him sprint into the darkness. That was the thing about Longlegs; you could drop him off anywhere in this city and he'd find his way without a problem; the streets and the people who habituated them were in his blood. Harry had no idea whether Longlegs could find the sort of men he was searching for but it was worth a try. At this point anything was worth a try.

Six

It was becoming more and more apparent that the Giants were going to capture the pennant; they were leading Pittsburgh two games to nothing and were prepared to make a clean sweep of it that evening. Everywhere you went in San Francisco the talk was about nothing but the Giants and their prospects for the Series. People were already leaping to the conclusion that Pittsburgh was out of the running.

Come evening, every radio, every TV set was tuned into the game. The whole damn city was on simulcast. By the second inning the score was tied, still nothing-nothing.

So preoccupied by the game were people that virtually no one paid attention to the report, broadcast at six on the evening news, that John Bull Ryan had done better than even the Giants by capturing 89.5 percent of the votes cast by the Brotherhood in its postponed election. His overwhelming majority was assured, the commentator had explained, because the dissidents, with no candidate of their own to support, had simply boycotted the election. The murders of Bernie Tuber and his family were mentioned almost as an afterthought. Harry felt like he was the only one in the city to remember them.

Although ostensibly he was still assigned to the case, so many leads had dried up, so many clues had proved unavailing that he was really left with nothing to go on. Which was why he was out tonight looking for Longlegs.

Longlegs might not be his last hope, but if he came up empty-handed then Harry wasn't sure where he'd go from there.

Longlegs was not hard to find. He was seated in a dive off Pacific, a dank place smelling of piss, booze, and failure. Like almost everyone else in town he was watching the ballgame on a color TV squeezed into a nook above the counter. Everyone clustered around the bar, shadowy forms in the harsh, grim lighting; it looked like one more straight gin would send them toppling over from their stools.

Harry approached Longlegs from behind and saddled up next to him. For about two minutes Longlegs pretended not to notice him, continuing to rest his eyes on the TV. But he knew very well that Harry was there. Longlegs might have fucked up at just about everything he tried to do in life but he was a survivor; he had the sense of a survivor. A nuclear holocaust or an ice age, it wouldn't matter; in the devastation, in the frozen wilderness the man would still be running his scams.

"Officer Callahan," Longlegs said, taking a sip from the shooter clutched in his hand. "How do you do?"

"What've you got for me?"

"Straight to the point. No wasting time." There was suddenly a lot of shouting in the bar. The Pirates had just succeeded in loading the bases. The crowd was roaring at the Giants' pitcher: "Take the son of a bitch outta there!"

Harry was not interested. Gripping Longlegs by the arm, hard so that he would feel it, he repeated his question.

"Because if you don't have anything for me I am afraid I'm going to have to take you in."

"Hey, lay off, man." Longlegs had the kind of plastic face that could express outrage with utter conviction. Harry's grip remained as taut as before. "Ok, Ok, I talked with some cats. I can't guarantee satisfaction, but I'm told they're some of the best in the business."

"How many?"

"Two. I didn't meet them personally. They are not

63

cats I want to be on intimate terms with, you catch my meaning? I went through a friend. A heavy dude."

"Where?"

Longlegs gave him the name of a bar near Fisherman's Wharf. The owner of the bar was reputed to have Mafia connections.

"Thursday, 4 P.M., the cat you want is gonna be wearing a red flower in his buttonhole and a red hankie in his pocket. He'll be waiting for you."

By four in the afternoon on Thursday Harry had managed to make himself look like a wealthy man, a little on the flashy side with a sportscoat a trifle too loud, glasses tinted an interesting shade of light chartreuse, white ducks, and a sporty blue cap perched on an abundance of blond hair that he'd fitted securely to the contours of the hair that was his by birth.

The bar where the rendezvous was to occur faced bayward, open to the sun and sea; there was a great big glorious sun in the west, spreading generous doses of light into the place. The bar was mostly inhabited by tourists and out-of work sailors who were looking for somebody to get them drunk and listen to their stories of fifty-cent whores they'd balled in the Far East.

There were a few cream-colored tables set out beyond the bar area, and at one of them was seated the man Harry wanted. As Longlegs had said, the contact had a red flower pinned to his lapel and a slightly less brightly colored handkerchief springing out of his breast pocket. He did not look like a hit man. He did not look like anything really; just a complacent businessman putting away a few too many to pass the afternoon.

"I'm Mark Kincaid," Harry said.

"Sit down, why don't you?" the man said.

"I was told you'd be with somebody."

"That's correct. He'll be along presently. My name, by the way, is Jeff. You'll want to be calling me something so you can call me that."

64

He spoke distinctly, with no trace of an accent so that it was impossible to tell from what part of the country he came. His eyes had a hazy, diffuse quality to them; they didn't appear to be focused on anything at all.

Harry ordered a drink and waited for Jeff to say something. But Jeff evidently had no intention of speaking until his companion showed up. His companion was shorter, paunchier than Jeff; he looked as though he'd recently undergone a face lift. No telltale lines of age could be detected at all. Both men were tanned, reflecting their apparent good health. Who knows, Harry thought, maybe a life as hit man wasn't as nerve-wracking as he would have suspected.

"This is Hank," said Jeff.

Hank nodded and pulled up a chair.

No one was anywhere around them. But Jeff wanted Harry to know that they could discuss their business freely here.

"What sort of arrangements did you have in mind, Mr. Kincaid?" Jeff was apparently going to do the talking for both men.

"Something fairly substantial. Something very clean."

"Ah yes. Clean." Jeff seemed to like the sound of the word.

"Like the Tuber hit a couple of weeks back."

Jeff allowed a slight smile to come to his lips. "I see. That kind of clean is going to cost you."

"I am ready to pay what's necessary."

Jeff seemed to consider this for a moment. "Necessary, Mr. Kincaid, might be in the neighborhood of two thousand."

"Per person?"

"Just how many did you have in mind?"

"Five." It was a figure Harry had pulled out of a hat. What he was doing, more or less, was improvising, playing it by ear.

At the mention of the number Jeff frowned. Hank's brow furrowed in sympathetic response with his partner. Killing five people seemed to displease them both.

"Five," Jeff repeated unhappily. "Mr. Kincaid, these five individuals, do you want them taken out all at once?"

"That's right. It was done with the Tubers."

"You keep bringing up the Tubers." It was Hank who spoke now. He had a gruff hoarse voice that was painful to listen to. "That was something special. You're talking about extraordinary circumstances when you're dealing with the Tuber hit."

Harry shrugged, leaning back in his chair, giving the impression that he hadn't a care in the world.

"You're telling me special is a problem?"

"Yes, that is what I am saying, Mr. Kincaid." Jeff was speaking now. "Five is a big problem."

"If it's a question of money . . ."

"Well, we're no longer talking five times two thousand, not for the job you want. It would have to be a much larger sum. Much larger. But money is not the issue here."

"If I understand what you're saying I'm talking to the wrong people."

There was a moment of hesitation before Jeff resumed. "I guess you could say that. In fact, I think I could safely say that for what you want you'd have to look beyond the local boys. I mean the free-lancers."

"The hit on the Tubers?"

"Outside. From what I hear the people they brought in on that were from Chicago, St. Louis. Hardcore folks all down the line."

"I see. How do I get in touch with them?"

Jeff held up his hand. "I'm not the yellow pages, Mr. Kincaid. You have to do that on your own."

"Well, can you tell me whether they're still available in San Francisco or do I have to go all the way to Chicago?"

"Oh, from what I hear—and it's just rumors we're talking about—but from what I hear there are a couple of

boys still around the bay area. They've got a new assignment the word is."

As offhandedly as possible Harry asked whether
they had any idea of what it was.

Jeff seemed to be deliberating as to whether he
should release this sort of information. Then he answered,
"From what I'm told there's a contract out on a cop
that's been giving somebody a lot of shit."

"A cop?"

"Detective name of Callahan."

Seven

The way Harry figured it, if what Jeff had told him was true, and he had little reason to think otherwise, he would no longer be obliged to search for the men who'd murdered Tuber and Meltzer. They would be coming to him.

His problem was in avoiding Tuber's fate and Meltzer's. His problem was also in taking at least one of these professional killers alive. Dead, they wouldn't be of much help to him.

The assumption that Harry went on was that they would attempt the hit when he was off-duty. To kill him while he was pursuing police business would complicate the situation. Most likely they would make it look like the result of an accident; equally as possible, he would be picked up, taken somewhere far away, and allowed to disappear permanently. Harry Callahan would be turned into a dim fading memory.

If Harry had suffered from paranoid fears before, if he was edgy, tense, and insomniac, he was worse now. Always on guard, he wouldn't even get into bed without making sure his .44 Magnum was within easy reach.

The days passed; they began to take longer than usual to end. And some days just didn't end at all. Sunrise would find Harry sitting at the kitchen table, slugging down coffee, waiting, waiting until he thought he would go mad. It was possible, he thought, that he had been misled. Jeff and Hank might have been told who he was and had deliberately lied to him. A form of psychological warfare: torture Callahan with doubt.

But he couldn't be sure. He had no way of checking the truth. No one out there, particularly no one on the force, was to be trusted.

His apartment in the meantime was beginning to resemble the battlefield of Verdun. It cried out for cleaning. Plates were piling up in the sink. The refrigerator was nearly empty and what food was in it was no longer fit for human consumption.

I must do something about this mess, Harry thought. He got himself a beer and did nothing.

It was Sunday now, a bright blistering Sunday morning. From the window of his apartment Harry could hear the neighborhood kids playing softball in the street. The sound the ball made when it was whacked by a bat was loud and abrupt enough to send the adrenalin racing in his blood. The way Harry looked at it, he must have already depleted most of the adrenalin he had in stock. Exhaustion was settling in, starting to dull his senses.

There was a knocking on the door, a barely audible tattoo. Harry's hand instantly sought out his gun. Still, he reasoned, it was not very likely that hit men would knock before they set about their task.

Nonetheless, he was real careful about how he opened the door, parting it an inch or so, while stepping back so as to avoid presenting a potential target.

"Hi, Harry, I came to see how you were doing."

The voice was demure and insinuating at the same time. The eyes were beautiful but disconcerting in the intensity of their gaze.

It was Keiko from downstairs. Harry let her in.

Lithe, with the grace of a dancer, she was attired as she usually was, in a loose, half-open shirt and jeans that clung avidly to her lean, finely tapered legs.

"God, it's a mess in here," she said, surveying the apartment.

"My assessment of the situation exactly." Harry

69

gave her a choice of beer or wine, the extent of the refreshment he had available. She opted for the beer, then immediately began to run the water and wash the dishes. "You need a woman's touch. Why don't you hire someone to come in once a week and clean this place?"

"It's an idea whose time has come."

"And gone. Where have you been? I never see you around anymore."

"I'm keeping strange hours these days."

"New case you're working on?"

"Old case, growing moldly by the minute."

"I think you need a vacation, Harry."

"That's what everyone tells me."

He looked toward the girl, admiring the way her jeans molded themselves to her soft pleasing rump. Keiko had once long ago been a lover but quickly realized that no lasting relationship would be possible with someone like Harry. She was now a friend, but one who was concerned and always eager to help—if Harry would let her.

But right now there was nothing she could do. Harry was devoted to the principle of taking action, getting the jump on an opponent before he could mobilize himself. But now he could do nothing but wait. That was the bitch of it. He strode over to the window and peered out. No sign of life. He could hear the kids playing softball but not see them. He wondered what had happened to the joker who'd been hired to follow him around town. Hadn't caught a glimpse of him for several days now. Was this a good omen or not? Truth was he didn't know.

Just as he turned to face Keiko the window exploded, glass showering him before he could get out of the way. Blood began trickling down from his scalp where a sliver of glass had lacerated him.

Keiko shrieked, not yet understanding what had happened. There was a second shot, a muffled detonation, and then an eruption of plaster from the opposite wall.

70

"Get down!" Harry yelled even as he threw himself down on the floor.

Keiko responded at once. Her voice betrayed her fear though she struggled to retain her composure. More plaster was thrown off the wall as the unseen sniper continued the fusillade.

"What's happening? What is it, Harry?"

Grasping hold of the holster slung over the chair, Harry removed his .44. Keiko raised her head to better see what he was doing, but Harry immediately forced it back down. He regretted that she had decided on this moment to come and help him with the housework. It was one thing if he got himself killed, but he couldn't bear the thought that a friend should be sacrificed through no fault of her own.

"Be damned if I thought they'd do it this way," Harry muttered to himself. He had not anticipated so brazen and relentless an attack. For a few moments there was silence; it was eerie, the silence you find in the eye of a hurricane. Outside there was a loud thump as a youthful batter connected. The sniper was using a silencer; the only noise came on impact inside of Harry's apartment. The rest of the world kept on as though nothing unusual were happening.

Keiko didn't dare speak. Whatever Harry told her to do she would do. Where they were both positioned, stretched out on the floor, there was no way that the sniper could hit them, not unless he could belly right up to the window and take aim. On the other hand, he could, if he wanted, keep Harry a prisoner in his apartment for as long as he cared to; the door was exposed through the shattered window. Should Harry and Keiko attempt to bolt, the assassin could bring them down instantly.

With difficulty Harry inched toward the table by his bed where the phone rested. There was no further fire, but it was Harry's feeling that the sniper was out there, undoubtedly enjoying his advantage in the situation.

Harry brought the phone down level to him and dialed his department.

He asked to speak to DiGeorgio but remembered that DiGeorgio was not on duty, it being the middle of a Sunday afternoon. He tried for Judson but Judson too was unavailable. So he had to settle for another colleague, Carl Pickney, with whom he was only marginally acquainted. As succinctly as possible he explained his predicament and was in turn assured that help would be forthcoming in minutes.

No sooner had he placed the phone down than his invisible friend opened up again. This time he found a target in a half-empty bottle of Red Label that had been a Christmas gift from the radio dispatcher. The bottle seemed to disappear into a thousand fragments, jettisoned to all points of the compass by a geyser of scotch. Shards of glass and drops of scotch rained down on them but did not do any harm. The scalp wound Harry had sustained earlier had stopped bleeding although he looked a mess.

"Next thing to losing my life, I hate losing a good bottle of booze," Harry said. He winced as another couple of shots tore into a mirror and sent it tumbling in a confusion of splinters to the floor.

The sniper seemed to be working according to some sort of schedule, three minutes on, three minutes off. But he varied this rhythm enough so that it was completely unpredictable. Perhaps he hoped that he would either catch Harry off guard or else get him so frustrated that he would risk exposing himself in order to retaliate. But there was really nothing Harry could do; no target presented itself. For all he knew, his assailant might be concealed in an apartment across the way or else be moving from one point to another.

"How long do you suppose he'll keep on like this?" Keiko asked, her voice reduced to a bare whisper.

"Can't be too much longer. There should be a backup unit here any moment. When that happens he'll run." Despite the confidence he tried to give his words he wasn't quite so certain. As the minutes passed, he began to seriously wonder whether he could rely on his colleagues to come to his assistance.

He reached for the phone and dialed again.

"Harry, everything's fine, we're on our way," Pickney told him. "Just hold on a minute longer."

A succession of rounds pulverized a swatch of the far wall. Plaster dust swept through the room in a cloud, causing both Harry and Keiko to cough.

"Hold on a minute longer the man says." Harry cursed Pickney for his complacent attitude; it stood to reason, he thought, Pickney wasn't the one getting shot at.

Right then there was a new series of reports, but they were originating from another direction altogether. Gruesome-looking holes had begun to appear in the door. But the sniper across the way wasn't responsible for them. Someone in the hall, directly outside the door, was.

"Shit. More trouble." And more serious trouble, too.

Meanwhile the sniper was continuing to lay down a barrage of greater intensity than before; undoubtedly this attack was being orchestrated by someone who wanted to make Harry sweat before finishing him off.

The lock on the door yielded gracelessly to a quick succession of shots that sent it flying, still in one clumsy metal piece, clear across the room.

Harry threw his body over Keiko's, sighting his .44, but refrained from firing. He did not wish to betray his position yet. If he was correct in his thinking the sniper outside and the man—or men—outside his door were in radio contact. But he was fairly convinced that he was out of the sniper's line of sight which meant that none of the attackers could be absolutely certain where he was in the apartment. The withering barrage was intended to lure him out but he wasn't playing by their rules.

And the attackers in the hallway did not have the

latitude the sniper did. They couldn't remain shooting out the door forever; they were sure to be spotted. Either they would have to move decisively or give up and go back to the drawing board.

Abruptly, fire from both positions ceased. It was only a brief intermission between acts though. One of the gunmen, more optimistic perhaps than his companions or else more foolishly confident of his abilities, kicked the weakened door open and almost at the same moment threw himself backward. Harry saw not his body so much as his shadow; instinctively, he gauged the distance to where the man was and fired twice. The man was quick all right but not so quick that he eluded Harry altogether. One bullet took him at thigh-level and since the .44 is one powerful handgun it had sufficient force to throw him against the opposite wall, blood spurting from his wound in such torrents that Harry assumed he must have struck an artery.

Keiko shrieked with terror and buried her head in her arms. There was a furious exchange of fire that while it lasted for only twenty seconds still seemed to resemble a full-pitched battle. The problem was, Harry had no idea of how many opponents he was facing. Two, possibly three, he figured. Evidently he had earned himself quite a reputation; a small army had to be sent to kill him.

Curiously, despite the number of shots discharged, the only injuries that were inflicted accrued to Harry's already devastated living quarters. Obviously the other assailants had no interest in following their companion's display of bravado.

During this fray the sniper had concentrated his fire away from the doorway rather than risk hitting his friends. So Harry decided to seize the opportunity. Cautioning Keiko to remain where she was, he sprang up and dived like a son of a bitch through the doorway, rolling over in a protective posture, the .44 extended in his hands. The sniper, caught unawares, sent several rounds whining ineffectually over Harry's head.

Except for the man he'd wounded, the hall was empty. Abandoned by his friends in their haste to get away, the enfeebled assassin was dragging himself down toward the stairs, leaving a long winding trail of fresh blood behind him. It was Harry's hope that he could take him alive.

Yet the hit man was not as interested in saving his own life as he was in taking Harry's. With surprising dexterity on the part of someone who'd been badly wounded he half-turned and fired his .45 auto Mark VI. But his balance was precarious owing to the injury and his grip too unsteady for his aim to be reliable. But since Harry was not about to give him the opportunity to readjust his stance or steady his aim, he felt he had no choice but to fire back. The hit man took the round full in the chest and seemed to vanish as he toppled down the staircase at the other end of the hall.

Harry moved quickly but cautiously, having no idea now as to the whereabouts of his other assailants. He gained the staircase, peered down to the landing. The fallen hit man lay sprawled out, his vitals spewing through the gaping hole the .44 had just produced. His friends were nowhere to be seen.

Above him Harry heard all sorts of commotion probably from his neighbors wondering why their building had suddenly been converted into a war zone; they'd always considered Harry a little strange but assumed that the presence of a police officer nearby would at least provide them with a sense of security. Obviously they would have second thoughts about that now.

With the way clear Harry raced down the stairs, leaping over the body there, prepared at any moment to confront the men who wanted to kill him. Keeping close to the wall, he was practically certain that his enemy would be waiting for him as soon as he reached the bottom landing. But this did not turn out to be the case. They had apparently fled.

Warily, he proceeded to the building entrance, drew

the door open so slightly that an observer would have to be scrutinizing it to notice the motion. But the opening he created was sufficient for Harry to get a good glimpse out into the street. He could see no one who posed a threat to him. In fact, the utter normalcy of the scene that greeted him was rather astonishing.

It was just then that a police cruiser pulled up across the street. Harry breathed a sigh of immense relief but was puzzled as to why there was only this one cruiser and no more. He had tried to make it clear that his situation was one that necessitated a virtual SWAT team.

The cruiser was occupied by only one man who presently emerged. Harry understood—or thought he did at any rate—why the reinforcement was so meager. The one man who had been sent to aid him was the last person in the world he cared to see. Sandy Patel.

Patel, looking unusually pleased with himself, sauntered across the street, his gait relaxed and assured. He could have been on his way to the circus the way he was walking. And while his right hand was close to his gun he had yet to make any movement to unholster it.

Harry, on the other hand, held his .44 Magnum within view. Allowing the door to open farther, Harry nodded to his colleague but his expression remained as blank as an Antarctic ice sheet.

With trepidation, Harry's neighbors advanced down the stairs, greeting the sight of the bloody body with gasps and muffled screams. Among them was Keiko, ashen-faced, her hands trembling. There were maybe a dozen observers in all; they stared at Harry as though he'd dropped in from Alpha Centurai. His face streaked with blood, his shirt and trousers coated with a dusting of plaster and unseemly scotch stains, his hair matted with some of those same substances, he presented a faintly grotesque, nightmarish appearance that he was, however, altogether oblivious of.

Patel regarded Harry with a mixture of astonishment and amusement. Harry had the sense that he had not expected to find him alive.

"Disappointed, Sandy?"

Patel pretended to be surprised by the question.

"I don't know what you mean," he said, looking past Harry.

"Oh, I think you do."

Harry directed him to where the hit man lay, his eyes still bulging open, expressive of the shock of his death. Blood had oozed all down the stairs making for a slick slippery surface.

Patel surveyed the damage, removing his dark glasses to do so. "Well," he said, "I suppose we should call downtown and get some help with all of this."

"Don't you think it's a bit late for that?"

Ignoring him, Patel stepped away and began walking toward the door.

Now that promptness wasn't any longer necessary, the police units showed up within five minutes of Patel's radio call. The whole street was cluttered with cruisers and two ambulances. But their arrival made no difference; neither the questions they put to Harry or the building's residents nor their concurrent surveillance of the surrounding area yielded any information regarding the assailants. More disappointingly, the dead man was found to have absolutely no identification on him.

At the end of an hour of questioning and unrewarding investigation on the part of his colleagues, Harry wearily trudged back up the stairs and returned to his apartment.

It was in shambles; the tables were overturned, the door was useless, the window was no more. And the floor was so covered with plaster, glass, and wood splinters that it could hardly be discerned beneath all the rubble. If a cyclone had torn through the place it could hardly have done greater damage. If he needed a housekeeper to restore order before, he now needed a four-man construction crew.

But more discouraging than the sorry state of his apartment was the realization that when he needed support the most his own department—or someone well-placed within it—had let him fight it out himself. Worse: someone had evidently set him up. Patel was part of it obviously, but he was a cog, an instrument. Well, he thought, he would have to work it on his own or else resign himself to the fate his would-be murderers had in store for him.

From the otherwise empty apartment that faced Harry's two men peered down at the policeman as he paced from one end of the room to the other, inspecting the wreckage. Every so often he would disappear from view but then, moments later, he'd come into focus again. At one point he stared through the shattered window glancing up in their direction but of course, he could see nothing that would alarm him. The shades were down in the windows; the strategic perforations that allowed the two men their view were too small to be discernible from such a distance.

The two men, while they shared the same profession, were as unalike in temperament as they were in the build of their bodies. One was tall enough to be the envy of any pro basketball team though he seemed not to know just what to do with his excess inches. For that reason, and simply to get into certain rooms and doors, he would keep his neck perpetually bent, with the result that his head appeared to be attached directly to his chest. He was quiet, withdrawn, and seldom quick to action. But he knew his business; killing he regarded much as a chef does gourmet cooking. His companion was of average height but squat and rotund with a fleshy face that, when anger leaked into his blood, became deep red. He was garrulous, impatient, and would sooner put a bullet into a friend than have to wait hours to kill an enemy. That he refrained from doing so was a testimony to his lust for money and his understanding that indiscriminate, unauthorized murder does not improve one's chances for a long happy life.

But since his objective now was to make certain that

Inspector #71 of the SFPD did not enjoy such a long and happy life he could not comprehend why he could not just pull the trigger the next time Harry stepped back into view and be done with it.

"We need orders," the taller one said, bored with having to explain over and over again.

"We had our orders before."

"But everything's changed now. The cops are everywhere."

"The cops are no problem."

"You don't know that. Some cops are no problem. Others are."

"What's he doing?" The shorter one still had his rifle—a German model Heckler & Koch G3SG/1, one of the finest sniper weapons available anywhere—aimed at Harry. But it was clear that what Harry was doing was moving out. Having thrown a few clothes into a suitcase, he was minutes from leaving. This meant that soon there would be no opportunity to make the hit at all. "I say take him out now. Right this minute."

The taller one was growing exasperated. "We wait. We don't work without new instructions."

It was then that the phone rang. Besides the two men, the phone was the only other occupant of this musty darkened apartment.

The taller one picked up. As he was better at delivering orders so he was better at receiving them.

The voice on the other end said, "Let him go. Your job is finished."

"He lives?" This surprised even the taller one.

"No, but we've chosen another strategy. You may be drawing too much heat so we want you to lay low for the time being. We've decided to employ someone else for the job."

"What's he saying?" the shorter one asked.

The taller one ignored him. He was offended that a substitute for them had been found. His professional pride was hurt. "We have him in view now. I want you to know we could take him with no problem."

"I am aware of that. But we're going with another party. No outside people this time."

"What do you mean by that?"

"I mean we're using a cop. One cop against the other." With that he hung up.

Eight

Although San Franciscans weren't following the Series with the same avidity they would have had the Giants not snatched defeat from the jaws of victory by losing the pennant, the Baltimore-Pittsburgh rivalry still excited a great deal of interest, especially in the dive that Longlegs favored. Warm as it was, this early October evening in San Francisco, it looked like it was tight-scrotum weather in Pittsburgh. A foul wind was taking the ball and playing around with it before giving it back to the men on the field.

Longlegs was enjoying this spectacle when he was grabbed roughly on the shoulder and spun around on his stool. When he looked up it was to see a cop.

He didn't know the cop's name but that wasn't important. He recognized him all right from the pawn shop. The blond with the 9mm Browning and the reflecting sunglasses.

While he did not know what was coming down, he suspected that it was nothing good. His neighbors in the bar shied away from him, sensing trouble. In his most lawless days, when you couldn't trust him with a dime, Longlegs had plenty of friends. But ever since the police had started getting on his case, people were staying far away from him. They acted as though he were contagious. Which, in a manner of speaking, maybe he was.

"I want to talk to you outside for a moment," said Sandy Patel.

"What is this about, man? I've been real good the last couple of weeks."

Patel didn't want to hear it. He got Longlegs outside and addressed him in a manner that left no doubt as to how serious he was.

"I want you to get in touch with your friend Harry Callahan. Tell him you have found out who the hit men are and set up a meeting."

"Hey, man, I don't know what you're talking about. I don't know nothing about no hit men."

Longlegs was shaking, his mouth was so dry he could barely speak.

Patel backed him into a corner, into the shadows outside the bar, then threw him against the trashcans. Groaning with pain, Longlegs sank to his knees. When he attempted to regain his balance Patel slapped him hard, sending him reeling. Patel believed in the preemptive attack.

"We know all about your dealings with Harry. Word gets around, my man. So I don't want to hear this shit. You refuse me and they are going to have to put you back together like a jigsaw puzzle just to fit you into a grave."

Wiping his mouth free of the blood that had gathered there, Longlegs cautiously got to his feet, at any moment expecting Patel to strike again and knock him back down.

"When you want me to do this?" Longlegs was hoping for a reprieve, a day or two, to give himself a chance to conveniently disappear.

"Right now. No sense wasting time."

Longlegs realized that it was useless to protest. Acquiescing to Patel's demands, he allowed himself to be hustled back into the bar and into the phone booth there. It was hard to hear; the booth was open, there was music pouring out of the jukebox and Howard Cosell's grating voice booming from the TV. Longlegs looked down at the number Patel had written out for him. His only hope was that Harry would not be in, but Harry was in all right, must have been sitting on top of the phone when he answered.

One look at Patel and he knew that he had no choice but to say what he'd been instructed to.

"Harry, look, I got some information for you. About those hit men you been running down. I got an idea who they might be."

"Which saloon are you at?"

Harry could hear the music and the sounds of the televised ballgame filtering through the wires.

Longlegs told him. "I'll meet you right outside," he said because that was his line and with each passing day he was becoming a better and better actor.

"I trust you are satisfied," Longlegs said, training his blurry bloodshot eyes on Patel.

"Partially." Patel smiled, but it was not the kind of smile Longlegs generally appreciated. "You carrying a piece with you?"

After the conflict in the pawnshop a gun was about the last thing Longlegs wanted to be caught dead with. He thought again about the nature of that phrase *caught dead with*.

When Longlegs said no, Patel nodded sagely and owned that that was pretty much what he'd suspected. "For that reason I brought along a present." He led Longlegs back outside again and only when he was certain that no one was anywhere in the vicinity did he reveal a cheap Saturday night special.

The ghost of his long-departed mother couldn't have terrified Longlegs more. For all at once he understood what Patel wanted him to do.

"Oh no, man. You're not asking me what I think you're asking me! You wouldn't want me to be offing Officer Callahan, would you now?"

"Exactly." Patel's voice turned soothing but there was a false note to it that Longlegs immediately picked up. "But I'll see that you escape. There won't be any problems afterward. You just make sure that you fire before he has a chance to anticipate you. And don't stop until you've emptied the gun."

Under other circumstances Longlegs would have burst out laughing; knowing Harry's reputation as he did he would never attempt to go one-on-one with him, with guns, fists, or Bowie knives if it came to that. But these were not laughing circumstances. Glumly, he asked what would happen if he should refuse to comply.

"I'll blow you the hell away."

"That's what I figured you'd say."

"It won't be as hard as you expect. Harry doesn't suspect you."

"Oh, I don't know about that. Officer Callahan, he suspects every mother that moves."

But Patel was a better judge of the situation than Longlegs had believed. Harry was so tense, so near the biting edge of exhaustion, that he was no longer humanly able to stay on top of things as he should. He materialized out of the San Francisco night like a man who's just emerged from a couple of months buried in a cave. He looked shot, dazed, but he still had a decisive walk, purposefully straight ahead.

"Over here, Harry!" Longlegs called to him.

The noise and music from the bar could be heard in this half-darkened spot where the bar's lights and the streetlamp broke off. The top of a garbage can clattered noisily to the pavement. Mice or else a cat was playing.

Longlegs' chest was heavy with fear; the pressure kept mounting, squeezing his heart until he thought the blood must be getting sucked all the hell out of it. The barrel of the Saturday night special was becoming ever more slippery with the sweat from his palm. Patel had told him to shoot right out of his pocket as soon as Harry came close enough to him. How close was close enough? At this point, a thousand miles for him was close enough.

Patel was in back of him, around the corner, out of sight and out of Harry's range. Longlegs couldn't see the glint of his Browning—wouldn't have dared shift his eyes to look in any case—but he knew it was there all right. If he failed to shoot Harry, Patel would shoot him. But he had the instinctive feeling that he would be blown away no matter what he did. The odds are always with whitey, he mused. Always.

Harry was approaching, closing the distance with some speed. Ten yards remained between them. Longlegs knew damn well he was going to do something quickly. It was one thing when he'd stuck up grocers and gas station attendants; he'd had the advantage and while he was afraid, they were more afraid. But with two cops it was a whole different story. They were professionals and Longlegs was out of their league entirely.

Suddenly Harry stopped. Maybe that sixth sense of his was operating. But he stopped, didn't do anything else.

Longlegs couldn't help it or maybe he meant to but right at that point his eyes slid ever so slightly rightward in Patel's direction and Harry picked up on it. The speed with which he reacted astounded Longlegs.

He went down, providing as small a target as he could, but he still had no idea where or who his enemy was. Out of the corner of his eye Longlegs saw that Patel had shifted just enough to get a view of Harry, but it was not clear what he was going to do. He might still be waiting for Longlegs to act. He surely had a contingency plan though in case Longlegs did not.

Longlegs, almost wholly immobilized, watched these two men who could not see each other as though he were no longer a participant but a spectator, waiting to see how the movie developed. Something in his mind was telling him that this was no fucking movie, but that something did not also inform him as to what precisely he should do about it.

Then Harry, without a word, beckoned Longlegs forward. Longlegs couldn't move. So Harry decided to. Move he did, back, practically zigzagging, still with his eyes on the unhappy snitch. Patel, rather than risk allowing his victim to escape him, drew himself parallel to the wall, still not exposing himself, and extended his Browning automatic to fire.

But Longlegs realized that Harry couldn't see his assailant yet. Ah hell, he decided, if he was going to die he might as well earn his death. He turned, facing Patel, expecting his body to become a home for several 9mm rounds within the next several moments. But to his astonishment, Patel, either because he was concentrating too much on Harry or because he was saving Longlegs till later, didn't react to his sudden movement.

Still with his hand gripping the Saturday night special—actually a 38-caliber Liana Especiala made for seven rounds—Longlegs pulled the trigger. He wasn't really aiming at any point in particular, just in Patel's general direction. The gun, when it discharged, bruised his thigh with its recoil, causing him to grunt with pain. A singed hole now appeared in his pocket, partially exposing the pistol.

Patel was clearly taken by surprise. He still had his Browning up, aimed at Harry, but when he fired the bullet went awry. Longlegs' shot had caught him in the groin and, upon entry, torn up much of his intestines. The expression on his face, beheld more easily now as he fell towards the light, was one of surprise more than pain.

But the shot he fired panicked Longlegs who had no idea that he'd been lucky in his shooting; he flattened himself out on the ground, waiting for his death which he felt sure must be imminent.

Harry, spotting Patel for the first time, had excellently positioned himself and had his Magnum leveled directly at his antagonist. But he withheld his fire for a moment, being reluctant to inflict harm on another cop, albeit a cop who had a decidedly unfriendly attitude toward him. Also, he knew he would have to answer to Bressler if he did so, and that could prove more than a little bit awkward.

And, in any case, from where Harry was crouched, behind the rear of a parked Ford LTD, he was not in any immediate jeopardy.

Patel staggered forward, propelled by the pain that, now having made itself felt, began to blossom, coiling through his vitals with venomous fury. His eyes were glazing over. No longer able to see Harry or place him with any degree of certainty, he looked for a more convenient target. Blood, in the meantime, was spreading copiously over his uniform and leaking down his legs.

Longlegs was doing his best to crawl away, but he could not avoid Patel's attention. "Motherfucking son of a bitch," Patel mumbled, cursing both Longlegs' betrayal and his own miserable luck.

With the choice of lying there and simply doing nothing or expending another round from his .38 Especiala, Longlegs decided that the latter made more sense. Patel shot at him, putting all his energies into the task, but Longlegs scrambled out of the way. Finding a great deal of difficulty in extricating the gun from his ruptured pocket, he kept it where it was and fired from thigh-level again and again. And yet again. He was firing like crazy, ignoring the constant slam of the butt against his hand and leg, not at all sure where all these bullets were going.

Where they were all going with deadly but inadvertent accuracy was into Sandy Patel. He would jump involuntarily but otherwise he seemed incapable of responding. The last thing that he expected to happen was to meet his death at the hands of this spade, and so he resisted its coming for a few moments more than he would have had it been a white man perforating him with bullets. But Sandy Patel was only human after all, and at a certain point, no matter how much will he had, there was no way he had of resisting the inevitable. Blood no longer oozed from the wounds, it positively erupted, and deprived of his strength, his ambition, his concentration, even his rage, deprived of everything in fact but an awful gathering pain, he succumbed, allowed the darkness to sweep over him, and collapsed, dead before his body pitched forward to greet the awaiting pavement.

Longlegs did not move. He kept expecting Patel to

arise and continue in his quest to kill him. He could not believe that he had been responsible for ending his life. Actually, he didn't want to believe that he'd done this because whatever else Sandy Patel was he was still a cop and murdering a cop, especially if you were black, was something you couldn't readily dismiss. Longlegs began to wonder whether it might not have been better had he been the one shot and destined for a secure place in the earth six feet under.

"You can get up now," Harry said, approaching him.

Longlegs saw that a number of the bar's patrons had forsaken the game on television for the more violent spectacle on their doorstep. They were curious but puzzled, as yet uncertain as to exactly what had happened.

Longlegs got to his feet, unthinkingly still holding onto the Especiala that Patel had given him to kill Harry. Without offering any resistance, he allowed Harry to lead him to his car. This is it, he thought with characteristic fatalism, this is where it ends for you.

A police cruiser, its red beacon flinging swaths of light along the darkened streets as it raced toward the bar, could be discerned in Harry's rearview mirror. But Harry paid no attention to it. He already had his car moving.

Finally Longlegs spoke, his voice filled with remorse. "Officer Callahan, man, you gotta know this was not my doing. I swear to you on my mother's grave—"

Harry cut him off. "You don't have to explain." He brought the car to a halt in a vacated area not far from where the railroad tracks ran parallel to the Embarcadero. "You know a place you can disappear to?"

Longlegs regarded him with bafflement. "What do you mean?"

"What I said." Harry was becoming impatient. "I want you to disappear. For a good long time."

"How long's a good long time?"

"Oh, five or ten."

"Weeks?"

"Years."

"This is my home."

"Not any more it isn't." He leaned across Longlegs and opened the door for him. "See you around," he said, at the same time slipping the Saturday night special from the black man's grasp. "Let me dispose of this for you."

Longlegs gave Harry one more questioning glance, then did as Harry had ordered. "I suppose I should thank you."

"Forget it," Harry told him. "Forget everything."

Nine

The dress (orange in color, modest in style) that Darlene Farley first chose was not the one she finally settled for. Blue silk was what she ultimately decided on, a clinging bold designer concoction that she thought would be just right for dancing the night through till dawn. The silk had nearly the same texture as a spring breeze and was just about as protective; one brusque movement in any direction would result in the exposure of a breast. From every angle it was the sort of dress that disclosed another interesting view.

The necklace that wound close around her neck and the gold bracelets that jangled a trifle too noisily on her wrists had just been removed from her safe deposit box that morning. She was not so security-conscious as Braxton, but he'd prevailed upon her to secrete her valuables. The problem was that she didn't really care if her jewelry and furs were lost, stolen, or somehow mutilated. But that was because she'd never paid for any of them.

The occasion for which she dressed so seductively and for which she'd squandered most of the day in preparation, deliberating over creams, lotions, scents, and clothes, was the debut of a new discotheque that was located in the Nob Hill area off California.

There was nothing quite so much that Darlene liked to do as dance, with the notable exception of the entertainment she did in bed. There was all this nervous energy she had and, aside from dancing until exhaustion stopped her, she rarely could think of a better way to work it out of her system.

Usually Braxton indulged her, occasionally even accompanied her to discotheques. But try as he might, he couldn't comprehend why people gave themselves over to music that he found by turn monotonous and aggravating. He preferred his old hangouts, male enclaves, where he and his cronies could fall back on the rites and conversational gambits that they'd been developing for years. Not that Braxton didn't like being seen, parading around with a nubile twenty-eight-year-old blonde on his arm, displaying his virile image to all of San Francisco. But when he did squire her about, it was to such established nightspots as the Starlite Lounge, Henri's, and The Penthouse. People under the age of forty were an enigma to him and while having Darlene around invigorated him he seemed to resent her youthfulness and did his utmost to keep her away from others who were equally as young. Especially men.

But because he was busy with union affairs he sometimes had to relent and let her loose. Better, he thought, that she should go dancing at some public place than seclude herself in a bedroom—her own or someone else's—where she could not be as easily monitored.

Accordingly, Braxton had arranged for escorts for her who had his personal approval. These escorts Darlene referred to derisively as eunuchs because, while they were all handsome and urbane, walking models out of *GQ* Magazine, they would sooner shoot themselves than lay a hand on her. Temptation might be awesome, but still they would refrain. They knew, and knew with the absolute certainty that Jehovah's Witnesses have about God, that they need only make a pass at her and they would suffer retribution. Getting fired would be the least of it. For if they were correctly reading the implication in Braxton's commands they might end up being turned into eunuchs literally, and not just metaphorically.

So they danced with Darlene and dined with her and

joked and were photographed with her for the *Chronicle*'s society page, but when they brought her back to her apartment at the evening's end they were chaster than a virgin adolescent on his first date.

There were times when all the jewelry, all the furs, all the expense accounts, all the attention and money did not make up for the frustration she felt. She regretted that men could not be miniaturized so that she could smuggle them back home in her pocketbook, then blow them up again to full size.

But there was the dancing to save her. In ten minutes Philip Lem, tonight's eunuch, was to come and pick her up. But when she saw her door opening she knew that it was not Philip. Couldn't be. Only she and Braxton had the key.

Matt Braxton stood at the doorway, dressed elegantly in a tux. He smelled strongly of English Leather.

Darlene gave him a perfunctory kiss. She did not like it when Braxton burst in on her like this with no warning. "Don't tell me," she said, barely concealing the annoyance in her voice, "you've made a change in the schedule."

"How did you guess?" Braxton had the complacent smile he wore on his lips whenever he exercised power. Over a union or a single woman it didn't matter, the smile appeared. "We're going to L.A. The limousine's waiting outside. Ten-fifteen flight on Air West."

"What's in L.A.?"

"What's in L.A.? I'll tell you what's in L.A. Mel Potter is in L.A."

"I should know who Mel Potter is?"

"You should. You should know a lot of things. Mel Potter is a big-shot producer. He's on the backlot of 20th Century-Fox. The man's got a million deals going."

"That's the only sort of person you admire, isn't it? A man who's got a million deals going."

Braxton chose to ignore her. He had no intention of arguing with her. He'd allotted exactly ten minutes to the task of persuading Darlene to accompany him and no more. "This man Potter, he's interested in doing a story about my life. About the rise of the union under my leadership. We never met. So—" Braxton took hold of Darlene's hands, "so he arranged for me to meet some of his friends at a late night party."

"Oh good. A late night party in L.A."

"Malibu. Beautiful view I'm told."

"Why didn't you tell me this before?"

"It just came up. It's been in the works but you know, baby, we're both busy men."

Having said all this, Braxton was certain he'd made his point. He was a bit troubled that Darlene wasn't showing more pleasure; he'd have thought she'd greet his news with genuine enthusiasm. How many women get to see their man portrayed on the big screen, after all?

"I'm not going," Darlene declared flatly.

Braxton frowned. "Of course you're going. Get your wrap."

"You may have forgotten, but tonight's the night Icon II is opening."

"Icon II. What the hell is an Icon II?"

"The discotheque, Icon II. It is opening tonight. Everyone is going to be there. Mike Nichols. Sam Spiegel. Anne Reed. Christine Ford. Francis Coppola. Everyone. At Icon II, not at your Mel Potter's shack in Malibu. It's your life he wants to do, not mine, so you go."

Braxton refused to sympathize; opening night, closing night, it was the same to him. What mattered was the party in Malibu and the chance that he might be immortalized forever, or at least so long as the celluloid containing his story held up. But before he had an opportunity to terminate this argument (his ten minutes were nearly up), the telephone, a touchtone pink Princess, interrupted them.

"It's for you," Darlene told him, holding out the receiver for him.

"What did you say?" Braxton shouted into the phone. Darlene knew that it was bad news; Braxton got a look to him whenever it was bad news and that look was certainly there now. "Patel killed? How the hell did that happen? What's this about some nigger? I don't understand . . . You're always giving me these bullshit explanations . . . I don't want to hear it. You're to get this cop out of the way . . . . Yes, yes, damnit, bring in the Chicago boys, that's what we're paying them for, isn't it? . . . You're asking me where they are? . . . you're supposed to know that . . . Let me think . . . All right, I know Bull's out of town . . . You try to delegate authority and everyone fucks up. Can't depend on anyone else but yourself." Braxton removed a small notebook from his inside jacket pocket and flipped through a few pages before locating what he wanted. "OK, they're in the Richelieu. On Van Ness. Nick Lesko and Patrick Passaretti. You give them the details . . . No, that's Passaretti. P as in Paul . . . You give them the details . . . Right, you make sure that this fellow Callahan is floating in the bay by tomorrow night. Enough's enough." He slammed down the phone. Bad treatment for a Princess.

Moving past Darlene, he said gruffly, "Let's go. We're late already." In his anger he had forgotten their argument of a few minutes before and so assumed that there was no problem whatsoever. Darlene was sensitive enough to Braxton's moods to know that further resistance to going to L.A. was not only pointless but unwise. In this state there was no telling what he could do.

Once again he had won.

The party in Malibu turned out to be every bit as dreary as Darlene had anticipated. For one thing, there weren't very many people; the party was more a small gathering composed largely of studio executives and their wives. Scarcely any glamour aside from one actor Darlene recognized from a soap opera that she watched regularly during the daytime. She asked him what was supposed to happen next on the series, but either he didn't know or else he was under orders not to divulge any information. This disappointed her. There was no one to talk to and you could spend only so much time admiring the Pacific Ocean from the deck that adjoined the producer's house.

Darlene tired of the shoptalk, and Braxton was so preoccupied by the discussion about this movie project and so flattered that she despaired of getting any attention from him. Instead she got looped, thoroughly intoxicated on some explosive punch concoction that people kept ladling from a big silver bowl.

All she could keep thinking about was the festivities she was missing at the Icon II. As the evening progressed, her mood darkened more and more, her anger took hold of her, and she became determined to somehow exact revenge on Braxton. It struck her with all the immediacy and surprise of a late afternoon summer thundershower; it was such a provocative and dangerous idea that came to her that she nearly burst into a fit of nervous giggles. At first she could not actually see herself pulling it off but as the hours passed, and as Braxton's ego became perceptibly inflated, his voice more and more boisterous in recounting anecdotes, the idea seemed to gain in plausibility. Yes, she concluded, it is possible to do this thing.

There was no need to excuse herself. No one would notice her absence. She slipped upstairs, found a bedroom, and without the availability of light managed to locate a phone. "Operator," she said, keeping her voice low, "could you connect me to the San Francisco Police Department. I would like to speak to an officer named Callahan. No, I don't know the first name. Just Callahan."

Ten

"Who did you say this is?" Harry asked.

"A friend," the woman replied on the other end. "Just a friend."

And she hung up.

Harry stared at the buzzing receiver in his hand as if in expectation that further enlightenment might be forthcoming.

Well, he thought, it might be worth checking out her information. The last time a call had come like this he'd nearly been lured into a trap and killed. He would have to remember to be more cautious in this instance.

The Richelieu Motor Hotel, situated on Van Ness at Geary, consists of an older five-story hotel building and a motel grafted onto it. The lobby is characterized by squares of blond wood; glass doors on one side lead to the darkened pool area.

Harry stepped up to the desk and inquired after Patrick Passaretti and Nick Lesko.

To his surprise, the man behind the desk seemed to recognize the names immediately. "Oh yes, sir. You must be Mr. Powell. Mr. Lesko and Mr. Passaretti are waiting for you inside of Zim's. That's right through the lobby. You'll find them seated inside at one of the tables."

Harry nodded in acknowledgment, wondering what the man's reaction would be when the real Mr. Powell arrived, an event he assumed would happen imminently.

96

Zim's Coffeehouse was open twenty-four hours a day which made it a convenient meeting place for insomniacs and drunks desperately in need of a restorative. It was close to two in the morning; Messrs. Powell, Passaretti, and Lesko kept late hours.

If you didn't know what to look for, Passaretti and Lesko would not attract any special attention. But Harry did know, and they stuck out like circus freaks—and while their sedentary postures bridged the height difference between them it was still obvious to Harry that a few inches in either direction and they could well be circus freaks—one a giant, the other a sad-faced voluble dwarf.

Harry took a seat practically across from their table. It was reasonable to assume that these were two of the men who had attempted to kill him in his apartment and who very likely were now waiting instructions so that they could rectify their failure on Sunday. Although they would only have to crane their necks to spot Harry, they had no special motive to do so. And Harry knew enough about human nature to realize that even if their eyes fell on him they probably would not make the connection that this, for Chrissakes, was the man they were supposed to hit. Not because they didn't have a clear idea of what their victim looked like but because they would not expect him here and as a result would overlook him. Harry was better at fading into the woodwork than they when he had to.

Ten minutes passed. And then the man he presumed to be Mr. Powell, a squat cigar-smoking character with a face turned beet-red by too much sun or too much booze or both, wandered in. He located Lesko and Passaretti right away and sat down with them. Harry was too far away to hear what they were saying, but he had a feeling he knew the subject of their conversation. Powell was someone who intrigued him. Powell was undoubtedly a minion of Braxton and as such he could provide the kind of link Harry had been looking for so long and futilely.

It was unfortunate this trio's discussion couldn't have been wired but that would be hoping for too much.

It was to escape just such clandestine scrutiny that they met in a public place like this.

Then Harry decided to try a bold experiment that would very likely lead to a lot more trouble than he needed. He was going to expose himself and compel them to take action. It was now time to emerge from the woodwork.

Yet he was anxious not to make it seem like he had caught on to them. They would be then confronted with a dilemma: on the one hand, maybe he was staking them out; on the other, maybe his being at Zim's at two in the morning was a pure coincidence. In either event Harry was operating on the premise that he would present them with too great a temptation to resist.

So he deliberately called attention to himself. Throwing himself into the role of a drunk who has had a few too many, he knocked his plate, still half-filled with a Spanish omelette, onto the floor. The crash resounded through the coffee shop, causing heads to turn. Harry pretended to ignore the curious faces peering at him.

When the waitress appeared, he told her the omelette was inedible, which was not the case at all. The waitress, who looked like she'd much rather be asleep, was justifiably indignant. "Sir, if you don't like our food you can let me know but that doesn't give you any right to throw it on the floor."

Harry gave her a disdainful glance and brushed past her.

"Sir, you still have to pay for your food." Under her breath she cursed him mercilessly.

Harry continued out of the coffee shop, dismissing her with a peremptory gesture. He reminded himself that when this was all over—if it ever did get all over—he would have to return and give her a good tip for taking part, however unwittingly, in this little charade he'd contrived.

As he made his way through the lobby at a very cautious pace, half-lurching in emulation of a man well in his cups, he tried to restrain himself from looking around.

There was no question that his victims had noticed him and the commotion he'd created—everyone in the coffee-shop had—but had they correctly identified him and having done that, decided to follow him? Ah, Harry thought, how could they not? Callahan too bombed to even see straight: it was like looking a gift horse in the mouth.

Instead of proceeding directly toward the lobby exit, Harry chose the door that led out into the deserted pool area. It would be assumed that in his intoxicated state he had mistaken one door for the other.

Although he heard someone shout at him, warning him that the pool was not open at two in the morning, no one attempted to impede his progress, such as it was.

He could hear footsteps in back of him but whose they were he had no way of determining. Not until he was at the pool itself did he allow himself the luxury of turning around.

Light was sufficient to catch a glimpse of yourself in the pool whose chlorine-blue water now appeared almost completely black. There were, however, enough shadows to get lost in. Which is exactly what Harry did.

But not quick enough . . . .

"Over there, I see him over there!" Passaretti was trying to keep his voice down but in the silence and the still warm air it carried anyway.

"Where?"

"There, there!"

"What's he doing?"

"I don't know. Looks like he's throwing up."

And indeed it did. Harry was standing, with his back partially turned toward them, his head lowered out of sight. To complete the effect he began to retch. In the meantime, he had his .44 Magnum gripped firmly in his hands.

"Take him now." Passaretti was speaking louder because he assumed that Harry, in his misery, would be unaware of any intrusive presence.

By his voice Harry had a fairly good idea of where Passaretti had positioned himself; he was just shy of the door to the lobby. Taking no chances, Lesko was walking away from him, moving to a point almost directly opposite Harry. His footsteps betrayed him but again, thinking that Harry was out of commission, he was less attentive to keeping them muffled.

Powell wasn't with them. The Powells of the world never came in on the front line of this kind of operation. He was no doubt waiting for a favorable report in the lobby.

It was a matter of timing. Harry moved a moment too soon he might lose them. A moment too late he might lose himself.

He retched once again so as to reassure his impatient assassins that he was still thoroughly incapacitated. Then he dropped, spinning at the same time. Two shots, scarcely audible because of the silencers the men were employing, slammed into the wall a couple of feet above his head. Harry fired three times in succession, twice at Passaretti and once in the direction of his friend across the pool. Having no opportunity to properly aim at Lesko, he had to content himself with distracting him.

In this he succeeded. Lesko had in his effort to reposition himself slipped on a damp patch of cement and was struggling to regain his balance.

Passaretti had been hit. Only one of Harry's two slugs had entered him but one was enough. On impact he'd been flung into the pool, creating a noisy splash. He was still alive, grappling desperately with the water to get back to the surface. The water was fast filling up with his blood and soon there was so much of it that you couldn't see what had happened to the little guy. He never did come up for air. There was nothing much he could have used the air for in any case, with one lung shredded and hemorrhaging like crazy.

Lesko meanwhile had gotten himself vertical again and was firing back at Harry or where he thought Harry should be because by stumbling, he'd lost sight of his target and now couldn't find him again.

Confusedly, Lesko began to circle the periphery of the pool, certain that Harry must be somewhere nearby but where? All at once he found out. The tip of a .44 pressed up against his head. No sense, he realized, in trying to turn around. No sense in doing anything but coming to a dead stop.

"Drop it."

Lesko obeyed. His handgun bounced on the cement and flipped off into the pool, joining Passaretti and his gun. There was nothing but a blood-red cloud in the water; it would be one hell of a surprise for the people who came out for a dip the following morning.

"Now walk."

Lesko walked. It seemed under the circumstances a reasonable alternative.

As they approached the door leading to the hotel lobby the door swung open. There silhouetted in the lights from the lobby was none other than Mr. Powell. Evidently he anticipated nothing but good news, for his cigar was still protruding from his mouth; he was puffing away on it contentedly.

He could not see Harry from where he stood since Lesko pretty much hid him from view. On the other hand, there was no way he could miss all the blood in the pool. He assumed that it had to be Harry's blood.

"Where's Passaretti?" he asked.

Lesko didn't react. Harry hadn't given him instructions and so he wasn't about to say a word, not with a .44 strategically placed to expel the contents of his brain.

"You can tell him," Harry whispered, having drawn up a .38 that he kept strapped about his ankle in reserve. With a pistol in each hand he was confident that Powell presented no threat.

"In there." Lesko nodded towards the pool.

Powell frowned. He didn't seem to have understood. "What the hell do you mean in there?"

101

"What I said. Passaretti's finished, caput."

He didn't sound particularly aggrieved.

Now Powell understood. He took a couple of steps backward; if the light were any better you could have seen how pale he'd gone.

"Stay where you are," Harry commanded.

Powell swore and turned and bolted. Or tried to bolt. Harry raised his .38 and fired a warning shot that stirred up the surface directly beneath Powell's feet. He leapt up, did a little aerial ballet, but being so close to the door he didn't stop.

Again Harry fired, meaning to catch him in the leg. But Powell was moving too fast, zigzagging like crazy, and so the bullet missed him. But it did succeed in scaring the hell out of him because in his effort to escape he bumped up hard against the glass, cutting his brow.

With Lesko in front of him, Harry rushed toward Powell. Powell, stunned by the collision, must have realized that his opportunity had eluded him. Tugging a .357 Magnum out of a holster that had been hidden by his jacket he fired back. This gun of his lacked a silencer and so made quite a powerful concussive noise that probably awoke all the Richelieu's sleeping guests. There was in response a spurt of water at the far end of the pool. Clearly, Powell wasn't much of a shot.

Harry, still using his smaller caliber gun, returned the fire. Glass shattered but Powell was not harmed. Almost simultaneously Powell got off another couple of rounds, better targeted this time. Harry by this point was nearly on top of him—with Lesko still between them, doing what he could to escape the crossfire. But it was not Lesko's lucky day. Hit in front he fell in the way of the .38 and was hit from behind. He screamed, then in an oddly graceful movement pitched forward into the pool.

Powell seemed to think that Lesko, in his death throes, would provide him with the distraction necessary to finally make it into the lobby. Now that the battle had come down to just him and Harry he realized that he'd better act quickly. If two professional hit men such as

Lesko and Passaretti could not kill Harry then what chance did he have? He could depend only on chance, and he knew that men who depended on chance didn't survive very long in this world.

So he turned and rushed headlong—this time avoiding a collision—into the lobby. For a moment he was convinced that he was safe; the well-lit interior was more reassuring than the partial darkness outside. That there were a scattering of people, guests and staff alike, who were observing his progress through the lobby in the general direction of Van Ness, that he still held his gun in his hand, did not occur to him. He was too busy escaping to notice such things.

Powell ran badly. He had no endurance; his lungs, so often filled with smoke, were not up to the task. He reached the exit out of breath. But he was grateful that he hadn't been pursued. Daring to look back into the lobby, he for the first time glimpsed all the curious onlookers but they, intimidated by the sight of his .357, were making no movement whatsoever; certainly they weren't about to stop him. But among them there was no Harry Callahan.

That was all that counted, that there be no Harry Callahan.

Powell stepped out on Van Ness. His car was parked too far away; he wasn't about to walk to it. A cab was pulling up; the back seat was empty and right away Powell hailed it and got in. At the same moment the door on the other side opened and a man slid in next to him. It was Harry Callahan.

Putting a .44 within inches of Powell's head and placing his .38 so that if discharged it would blow Powell's balls into the stuffing of his seat, he said very quietly, "You're it," thereby ending this particular game of hide-and-go-seek. Powell, recognizing the futility of resisting further, agreeably surrendered his gun.

The hack, who'd witnessed the tag in his rearview mirror, had yet to say a word, no doubt greatly disheartened to see all this artillery and men willing to use it sitting in his back seat.

"I'm a police officer," Harry announced, adding that the hack would just have to take it on faith since he couldn't very well get out his badge with both hands occupied. He directed the unhappy driver to headquarters, then turned his attention to his prisoner, handcuffing him. "Now, Mr. Powell, just so this is all kosher I'm going to read you your rights."

"And then?"

"And then if you don't start answering the questions I'm going to ask, you just might end up envying your friends Passaretti and Lesko."

Eleven

The assistant D.A. couldn't have been more than thirty-five years old; he had the look of a Harvard Law grad who'd trained in the Southern District of New York, done some *pro bono* work, and somehow decided he'd be better off coming west and setting up shop on another coast altogether. Now it might be he was raised right here in San Francisco, but the impression Harry had was of someone who'd breathed the salt spray off the Atlantic Ocean until some dormant restlessness had sprung up in him and got him moving.

He still gave off an Ivy League aura; he was tall and not bad looking, but too serious in his bearing. He wore glasses that had a tint to them which subtly altered depending on how much light there was available and he dressed impeccably. His name was Robert Nunn. He beckoned Harry to a seat in front of his desk.

"Officer Callahan, I have been studying with great interest your report about the whole Tuber case," he began, allowing his fingers to dance through a great sheaf of papers on his blotter.

Harry said nothing, waiting to hear that the evidence was so slender that it was not worth the State's time and money to prosecute. Or else that the confession he'd elicited from Justin Powell was somehow unconstitutional and thus inadmissible in a court of law.

"You've been working on this for months now haven't you?"

Harry owned that he had.

Abruptly Nunn rose. "I like it," he said. "I like the work you've done. I think we may have a problem with your promise to Powell. I'm a little disturbed, I don't mind telling you, about the way you promised him immunity without clearing it with our office—" He put up his hand, uninterested in the protest he anticipated from Harry. "But that's neither here nor there. I think we can work something out with our man Powell. The important thing is to get to Braxton, is it not?"

For the first time Harry regarded him with something other than skepticism and mistrust. Was it possible that he'd found an ally—and in the D.A.'s office of all places?

"I agree with you but you'll notice Powell never named Braxton. He charged only that he'd received orders from Ryan and that all he did was to deliver them. That's the way it's always set up. Bull and Powell, they're errand boys. They got power till Braxton snaps it away from them."

"I am aware of that." Nunn removed his glasses and rubbed his eyes. Without the glasses he looked slightly haggard as if he hadn't slept well for weeks. "But I don't think that we're facing any serious obstacles here. I've obtained a warrant for Ryan's arrest. Since you seem to have such a pronounced interest in this case I wanted you to know about the warrent. Maybe, if you're lucky, you'll get to do the honors and serve it. I'm not in charge of that department." He smiled at Harry. There was something more than he was revealing here, Harry knew. But he was willing to wait for it.

"The strategy of this office, I should think, would be to play one man against the other. Divide and conquer, right? Powell takes us to Bull. Bull takes us to Matt Braxton."

"How do you figure? Bull's scared shitless of Braxton."

"I think we can persuade Bull. I can't guarantee it but suppose we tell him he can walk. The Grand Jury hands up a sealed indictment maybe. But maybe not. Maybe something goes awry and we have to drop the case. Just so we go easy with him. But at the same time we tell him he can control the Brotherhood, really control it. Like Fitzsimmons got to do with the Teamsters once Hoffa was sent up. I think Bull will go for it. It must be humiliating for him being a puppet. Braxton's what, in his mid-sixties? Something like that. A guy like that, Christ, he can hold out for decades. Years and years, and Bull's sitting on his ass, his hands tied, can't take a leak unless Braxton says yes. We play on that, and I think we have something."

"I want to ask you a question. I like what you're saying but there's something I figure you're holding back."

Nunn shrugged. "Holding back's my business. What's the question?"

"The D.A., Pritchard, where does he fit into this scheme of things? He dream this up with you or have you been doing a little homework on the side?"

Nunn rubbed his chin thoughtfully, sat back down again, and started rocking in his chair. It was not a chair made for rocking and it almost seemed like he was going to topple right over. "Interesting question, Callahan. James Pritchard is an able district attorney, of course, and in the last year here I have received a considerable legal education under his guidance . . ."

Although Harry wanted him to cut the bullshit he recognized how under these circumstances such formalities were necessary; Nunn could not call into question his superior's capabilities in front of an investigator for the police department.

"I don't know whether you are aware of it or not," Nunn continued, "but Mr. Pritchard is attending a special conference on law enforcement in Tokyo. He will be gone for another couple of weeks or so. He has decided to take a little vacation once the conference ends. He's got a lot of time coming to him and he well deserves it."

"So you're in charge of this office until his return?"

"We stay in touch by phone naturally but yes, to answer your question, essentially I am in charge."

"And Mr. Pritchard knows of your strategy in regard to this case?"

Nunn hesitated for a moment that went on a little bit too long.

"Let me assure you that the District Attorney has been and will continue to be kept thoroughly abreast of every development in this case. I would not take one step without being absolutely certain that I had his sanction."

Two possibilities occurred to Harry; either Nunn was making this move on his own, taking advantage of his superior's absence to further his own ambitions, which Harry could sense were considerable, or else he had the tacit approval of Pritchard who rather than be held directly responsible wanted to be far out of town when the shit hit the fan. Whichever was true it didn't much matter to Harry. So long as the D.A.'s office would get behind him.

"I'm told that if Braxton or Bull or any of the Brotherhood's top leadership gets put away there's going to be a dock strike."

"And where did you hear that?" Nunn kept his voice even.

"These things get around."

"The Brotherhood ratified a new contract last year. Any strike would be illegal and our office would view it with gravity. You know, Callahan, that the penalties we could impose are very stiff. The State has its own arsenal." Nunn stood up, ending the interview.

"Just one more thing."

"Yes?"

"This isn't just for some publicity, is it? Everybody gets his picture in the papers, then goes home on bail half an hour later, and the whole thing dies?"

"Not at all, Callahan. This is for real. We're in dead earnest."

Whatever Nunn's demurrals, it was apparent that publicity wasn't the last thing on his mind either. For when police swooped down on the Brotherhood's office at midday, only hours after Harry's briefing, the press was out in force. Photographers swarmed around the building's entrance, anxiously awaiting the imminent appearance of the suspect.

The suspect, John Bull Ryan, had had, until a few minutes previously, no idea that he was a suspect. The first he'd learned about it was when a *Chronicle* reporter had phoned him and asked him what his response to his arrest was. "No comment," he'd answered curtly, hanging up.

Instantly he was back on the phone. As he always did in such exigent situations he called Braxton for advice. Braxton would know what to do.

"Give me time, I'll get back to you," was Braxton's succinct comment when informed of the situation.

"Time! There is no goddamn time. The police'll be here any minute."

"Nothing I can do about that. Listen, Bull, we'll get you out of it. You're not going to have to do time, take my word for it. The Brotherhood's flush. They'll set bail, we'll pay it, then we'll work it out."

"What went wrong, Matt? What went fucking wrong?"

"I honestly don't know, Bull. But I'll find out, I promise you."

"It wasn't supposed to get this far."

"You don't have to tell me," Braxton said, putting an end to the exchange.

Panic was spreading inside of Bull, like a poison contaminating his blood. It was a panic he'd felt before but many years ago, when he'd been arrested on the docks, bloody and half-blind with pain from police truncheons. But at least then he was not alone; twenty others had been taken into custody along with him. Now there was just him. And despite Braxton's assurances, he wasn't certain that he hadn't been set up by Braxton to begin with. Although they hadn't had any serious disagreements, that wasn't a guarantee that he was safe. Braxton could have decided that with Powell's arrest things had gotten too far out of hand and that a scapegoat was needed.

Outside there was some sort of commotion. His secretary was arguing with someone. The police no doubt. Bull seated himself, combing what hair he had remaining to him; at the very least he wished to look presentable, still in command . . .

A couple of minutes passed. The door to his office was opened and in walked four uniformed officers led by a man in plainclothes. He recognized the man in plainclothes. It was Harry Callahan.

He rose to greet his unwanted visitor. "You're a lucky man, Callahan. You should never have made it to this point." He barely glanced at the warrant Harry held out for his inspection. "You know you're not going to keep me."

Harry shrugged. "You know," he said, smiling enigmatically, "you may be right."

The manner in which he said this disconcerted Bull. Now he was truly worried.

As soon as news of Bull's arrest was made public, first on radio newscasts, later in the afternoon editions, Braxton released an official statement, asserting that he was certain Bull was innocent, while at the same time accusing the San Francisco Police Department of a malicious "witchhunt." "Unable to find the real murderers of Bernard Tuber and his family, the police in desperation have resorted to Gestapo tactics to convince the public they have solved the case," he maintained. He also hinted that politics was somehow involved. "There are elements," he went on, "that want to see the Brotherhood dismembered and destroyed. The Brotherhood, its leadership and members, wants to go on record in saying that if

110

the police and the politicians persist in this witchhunt, the economic well-being of this fair city may be placed in jeopardy." The implication was clear; keeping Bull locked up and pursuing the indictment against him—and anyone else in the union—might lead to a dock strike.

Not satisfied with this official statement, Braxton ordered the firebombing of a warehouse not far from the docks. It was chock full of fruit and cotton that had just been offloaded from a freighter with Panamanian registration that had done a shuttle run from the west coast of South America. Fire fighters required eight hours to extinguish the blaze that at times threatened other structures in the vicinity.

Braxton, when asked for a statement the following morning, met with reporters in his office, two floors above the one that Bull had occupied. He directed the reporters to his office window, which yielded a better view of the bay than his successor enjoyed, and gestured to the north. Ugly black smoke was welling up into the sky. The fire, while brought under control, had at that point still some hours to run.

"Of course, gentlemen, to my knowledge, no one in the Brotherhood had anything to do with that fire over there. I know what they're saying. They're saying it's arson, but so far we have been offered no proof of that. It is my contention that the Brotherhood is being framed. I don't want to name names. In fact, I'm just as much in the dark as you are. But you're reporters. You investigate. I put up fifty thousand dollars for the arrest and conviction of the murderer of Bernie Tuber. Would I do that if I thought my worthy successor Bull Ryan had any hand in it?" He leapt to his next sentence, uninterested in obtaining an answer to this. "But I'm serving a warning now that as much as I deplore acts of violence, against persons or property, I can well understand the emotional distress the membership must suffer from when something like this happens."

"You mean the warehouse burning?" a Hearst reporter asked.

"I mean the unjustified arrest of Bull Ryan," Braxton said, dismissing the newsmen from his presence.

Early that same evening the man in question was led into a windowless interrogation room at police headquarters, given a chair and a cigarette, and requested to sit.

His wait was not long. In a few minutes Harry appeared and took a seat opposite him.

"Are they treating you all right?"

"You care about my welfare?"

"Absolutely. You're very important to us right now."

Bull wondered just how important he was to Braxton but decided to say nothing.

"You ever hear of a fellow named Nick Lesko?"

"Never."

"Patrick Passaretti? The name mean anything to you?"

"No. Should it?"

"What about the phrase, 'the Chicago boys?' "

"I don't know. Is that what they call the White Sox?"

"Cute." Harry knew that they were only going through the motions, but it was a game that had to be played. "Clay Meltzer, you recognize the name?"

"Yes," Bull answered evenly, "he was in the employ of the Brotherhood."

"When he was killed was he still in the Brotherhood's employ?"

"He was."

"Why do you suppose he was killed?"

"I have no idea."

"Didn't the Brotherhood order him killed because he was about to implicate you and Braxton in the Tuber slayings?"

"That's your version, not mine."

"The way it is now, Mr. Ryan, we're going to pin you with five murder counts and at least one attempted murder."

"Oh yes? And who was the intended victim of this attempted murder?" Bull, expecting to be bailed out at any moment, was not bothering to take any of this seriously.

"You're looking at him," Harry said.

"Then I can only regret that the attempt failed in that case." He smiled. "Nothing personal."

"Of course not. What I'm saying is that you're going to hang for Matt Braxton. Unless—"

"Unless?"

"Unless you decide to cooperate."

"And turn State's evidence?"

"That's right."

Bull laughed. It was a quick, unpleasant laugh.

"You take me for an ass, don't you? Until I have a lawyer I have nothing more to say."

"Think it over."

Bull obviously had no intention of thinking it over. But before he could be led back to his holding cell, Harry had something to add. "You want to be careful, Mr. Ryan. From now on in you'll be wise to look over your shoulder wherever you go."

Bull frowned. "Why do you say that?"

"Because like your associate, Mr. Powell, you're a liability now. Word gets out you're cooperating with the D.A.'s office no telling what will happen."

Bull's face had gone ashen; in a matter of seconds he seemed to have aged years.

"You son of a bitch," he muttered, then turned from Harry. "You're way over your head, you know that, don't you? You know that?"

And in a sense Harry did know this; that he'd gotten this far surprised him. There was still a rabbi somewhere, probably in the department—Patel's control—who was watching out for Braxton. If Harry didn't act fast he would lose the whole ballgame; Braxton would slip out of his fingers, Bull would walk, and Powell, if he was still among the living, would repudiate his testimony. Even with Nunn's support Harry couldn't be certain he'd make

113

any further progress, not without a little unauthorized improvisation of his own.

Two hours later a Federal judge set bail for Bull at one hundred thousand dollars. A lawyer for the Brotherhood, a balding man with the aura of an ambulance chaser about him, posted it promptly. John Bull Ryan was out on the streets again.

It was a little after nine when the limousine—one of those Lincoln numbers, a block long with a sunroof and champagne in the cooler—conveyed Bull back to his home in Sausalito. Bull was tired; actually he was rather surprised to discover how exhausting his day in prison had been. Consequently, he'd declined an invitation extended by Braxton to have a celebratory dinner. What was he supposed to celebrate? His release on bail? By this point he had the feeling that he would soon be back in the slammer. Fail-safe devices weren't working any more and he didn't know why. What the hell purpose did it serve to pay out so much cash in protection money if he could still be allowed to twist slowly, slowly in the wind. It was a humiliating predicament, and Bull hadn't an inkling as to what he should do about it. He would see Braxton tomorrow morning but he already knew what Braxton would tell him: Forget it, we'll take care of everything, nothing to worry about, just get back to work. To save his own ass, Braxton would easily cut him loose—particularly if he thought that Bull was going to betray him.

It was developing into a real war of nerves—who would move first? And it had the effect of draining Bull completely.

The house he owned in Sausalito was a beautiful two-story edifice that rested a bit precariously on a steep gradient overlooking the honeycomb of houses and stores that composed the commercial center of the town. It was a spacious house with ten rooms; a comfortable place for a family. But the problem was there was no family. Bull's wife had taken his three kids and left him six years before, declaring that he was faithless to her and only loyal to Matt Braxton.

This was not quite the truth; he was rarely unfaithful to her—and then only with some one of those hookers that worked big city conventions. But he was hardly ever at home; he was no husband, still less a father. She'd been right to leave. But now what was he left with? A big house and a woman who came in a couple of times a week to clean.

He was too weary to prepare a meal for himself. He figured he'd drink it. Hell, that's all he wanted to do now, get loaded, watch the tube, and let a pleasant alcoholic oblivion overtake him sometime before day came in through the rectangular picture window that gave him a better view of Sausalito than he really wanted.

He was just settling into his armchair when there was a strange knocking sound against the side of the house. Bull stiffened in his chair, darting his eyes back and forth across the room. His ears perked up, anticipating another sound. But when it came it wasn't from the side of the house. No, this sound was the noisy clatter of glass as a bullet displaced it from the picture window.

Bull looked to the window. A jagged hole was there now and a stiff breeze blowing up from the bay was penetrating it. At first Bull couldn't understand what had happened. His brain was reacting too slowly; his exhaustion and the growing impact of the whiskey he was drinking were cutting down on his reaction time.

However, a second round, better aimed this time, did have the effect of arousing him. More glass was broken and blown halfway across the room as the bullet thudded into the armchair. Bull dived clumsily to the floor. A third shot took out the lamp, piercing its shade, splintering the bulb, and throwing the room into darkness.

Bull lay sprawled on his carpet, breathing hard; a painful rasping emerged from his lungs, he could barely swallow. Sweat popped out on his face and from under his arms. Something on the other side of the room exploded loudly. Although he couldn't see what it was, Bull guessed that it was the antique Chinese vase. Pity, it had

115

been worth a small fortune. He dared not move. Even after an hour had passed he remained where he was for fear that the assailant was still out there or—who knows?—might have decided to circle around and break into the house in order to complete what he'd started.

It was only when the first dim gray light appeared through the broken picture window that Bull allowed himself the luxury of picking himself up off the floor. The attack was evidently over. He first retrieved his whiskey. The ice had long ago melted but the drink still had its potency. Bull swilled down what was left, then went to the phone.

But as soon as he'd picked up the receiver he realized that he did not know whom to call. Braxton? It was probably Braxton who had engineered this assault against him. He had to do something, but for the next two and a half hours—while the sun inched itself up in the eastern sky—he found himself completely immobilized, unable to make any decision at all. Finally he dialed a number.

"I want to speak to Harry Callahan," he said. He waited until Callahan came on the line. "This is Ryan here. I want to tell you a little story if you got a minute."

Twelve

Once again the press was called out, a small restive army equipped with tape cassettes, 35mm Leicas, and mobile video units. This time they were summoned to a quaint gaslit street in the Cow Hollow district on Union Street. Right off it, on a mews, looking more like the creation of a confectioner than an architect, was a Victorian-influenced house, replete with an elaborately ornate roof and gingerbread facade. There was a boutique nearby, and both customers and proprietors were emerging from it to see what all the excitement was about.

Although a great deal of Matt Braxton's life was lived out in the open, in full view of the public, not many people knew where he made his home. This was information that was withheld not only to protect the Brotherhood leader's privacy but also because a charming, restored Victorian house didn't exactly fit the tough aggressive image that Braxton wished to propagate. This was his retreat, where he went to sequester himself against the intrusions of the world; other times he used an apartment near Jackson Square, right in the heart of the city's business district.

For John Bull Ryan, four uniformed men—plus Harry—had been recruited to make certain the arrest was carried out with no difficulty. For Matt Braxton, there were eight, including another plainclothes detective.

It was known that Braxton was usually guarded, at

117

least by two men who kept the mews under discreet surveillance whether or not the retired union leader was at home. But their responsibilities did not call for their holding off the police. All they could do was to dash up the stairs into the house, presumably to ask for further instructions. It had been many years since Matt Braxton had last been arrested and that was when he was a militant agitator down on the docks. Not the same situation at all.

Braxton, viewing the gathering forces from his bedroom window on the second floor, was more stunned than he was angry; having convinced himself that he was forever immune to arrest, he could not suddenly alter his state of mind to adjust to reality.

What particularly infuriated him was that Bull obviously had turned on him. It shouldn't have happened. There was no reason for it. Sure, someone had shot out his window and scared him shitless, but no one from the Brotherhood had been responsible for that; he'd given no orders to instigate a campaign of terror against Bull. What would have been the point? He would have had Bull killed and be done with it. Not that he hadn't considered doing so; it was just that there were already too many bodies. One more, he'd felt, he might have run out of luck. Well, he'd gambled and lost. It had happened before.

The door to the bedroom was opened; the bodyguard standing directly outside nodded to him.

No words were necessary. "Hell, invite 'em in."

Although he'd done his best to ensure Harry's death he was not unhappy to see him now. Here, he thought, was an antagonist worthy of his attention. He was tired of enemies he could easily vanquish.

Brushing aside the warrant that Harry proffered to him, he said to him, "Callahan, I have a question I want to ask you." When Harry refused to reply he went on. "Tell me something, did you shoot out that poor fucker's picture window in Sausalito? I sure as hell had nothing to do with that."

118

Harry looked at him directly and smiled. "Now why would I do a thing like that?"

Braxton laughed good-naturedly. "Yeah, why would you? Shit, why would you go and do something like that? Callahan, I want to tell you something else. You've done better than I thought anyone could. Honest to God. But I promise you you are going to get fucked. I mean you are beyond redemption, boy. And I am going to have one hell of a time doing it."

"But not this afternoon."

"No, you're right about that. This afternoon I'm the screwee. Later on we change positions."

Braxton assumed naturally that he, like Bull before him, would be back out on the streets by the time the sun set that day. But he had not taken into account one thing. Bull was still president of the Brotherhood and although he was lying low, hidden in some corner of the city, fearful of retribution from Braxton's allies, he still exerted control, for all practical purposes, over the organization. His signature was necessary for the disbursement of any large sum of money from the Brotherhood's treasury. And he had no intention at all of authorizing the money required to spring his predecessor on bail. So Braxton stayed in the jug.

By now much of the shock had worn off and there was in its place simple, blind fury. He raged in his cell; no longer able to content himself with visions of future vengeance, he was driven by the need to do something quick and decisive immediately. And since, even in jail, he was not altogether powerless, he realized that it was only a matter of time before the opportunity presented itself.

Since Matt Braxton was no ordinary prisoner he was treated especially well. He had a color television and radio and all the books he wanted at his disposal; a shower, if he wanted it, was his every morning. His food, superior to the fare served the other inmates, left him with little in the way of amenities to complain about. The real problem was that he was kept in isolation.

119

Warders, detectives, prosecutors, lawyers, and guards could see him, but no one from the prison community. But that did not mean the other prisoners didn't know he was there nor did it mean that they couldn't communicate back and forth.

And so inevitably Braxton got the word out: Shut down the docks. He was determined to show the City of San Francisco—and especially Some Fucking Police Department (SFPD), as many of its detractors called it—that they could not expect to take on Matt Braxton and win.

But Braxton's word was no longer Law; that was the sticking point. Half the union membership, the older half, was willing, as always, to comply with the boss's command and walked off the job. The other half, owing its allegiance to whomever controlled the Brotherhood at the moment—in this case Bull—chose to continue working. Ironically, the same dissidents who'd supported the late Bernie Tuber now found themselves allied with John Bull Ryan.

The stage was set for violence on the docks of the bay.

Thirteen

Bressler wasn't altogether happy with Harry. Not that he was ever exactly *happy* in general, but Harry particularly irritated him. He irritated him when he, for whatever reason, failed to solve a case or else left a lot of loose ends hanging. But he certainly irritated him more when he successfully brought a case to a close. Bressler was intelligent enough to recognize how irrational this line of thinking was, but somehow he couldn't bring himself to act any differently toward Harry. It was, he decided, something chemical; they belonged on different planets, that's all.

A week after Braxton's arrest he called Harry into his office.

Harry waited impatiently for Bressler to address him. He figured that his superior had found something else to criticize him about. But this time Bressler had nothing to complain of; instead, he had a new assignment for Harry. New, but still related to the Tuber case.

"You've heard about what's going down on the docks," he started.

"It's hard to miss."

"We have every reason to suspect it's going to get worse before it gets better. Now one of our difficulties is that we don't know who is organizing the wildcat strikers. But the violence seems carefully orchestrated—the brawls, the firebombings, the sabotage."

"Braxton. He's behind it."

"You have an obsession about this guy, Harry. Wh
you're saying is speculation. Remember, just because he
in jail now doesn't mean anyone's convicted him."

Harry remained sitting in stony silence.

Bressler relented. "Well, say, for the sake of arg
ment, that it is Braxton. He's not on the docks himse
Someone has to be his eyes and ears. Who? What I'd li
you to do is infiltrate the area, see what you can dig u
see if you can't identify the go-between."

Before Harry left Bressler called out to him: "A
Harry, watch yourself. Those longshoremen, they pl
pretty rough when they're angry."

Harry couldn't help smiling. Bressler expressing co
cern for his safety? The man must be going soft.

The bar that Harry stationed himself in was the sc
of dark derelict place that even Longlegs would ha
avoided. The men—and the few depleted hookers—th
hung out here had the look that comes from years
drink and bitterness; you had the feeling that anythi
could touch them off, even under the best of circu
stances. Killing was an option barely worth a seco
thought.

Harry was tall, and strong, but in comparison
some of these customers he appeared almost diminutiv
With their sinewy arms festooned with fading tattoos a
their pectoral muscles straining hard against their we
worn T-shirts, they made for intimidating presenc
Their capacity for booze was formidable. But it w
nothing to their anger; they were men who hated with
vengeance.

For this was a bastion of Braxton adherents. T
bar's clientele was enraged that their man should ha
been put in jail. Even if he did order the execution
Tuber and the others, well, that was all to the good,
their estimation. Tuber was a son of a bitch who had
coming to him.

Had any of the men known that Harry was direc
responsible for Braxton's arrest they would have wast

him right there and then. But they did not know so they contented themselves with isolating and patronizing him because whatever he was, he was an outsider who didn't belong and if he wasn't a cop then he probably was one of Bull's men.

Usually no one would talk to him. It took nearly half an hour for the bartender—an ex-longshoreman himself—to serve him. But by the fourth day he'd come into the place, at least one customer was curious enough—and inebriated enough—to entertain notions of speaking to him.

He was a shortish fellow actually, unshaven, half-blind, a veteran of a good many wars on the docks. He sidled up to Harry. "Who the fuck are you?"

"I'm a shipping investigator."

"The fuck you are."

"Don't believe it, same difference to me."

"Never heard of a shipping investigator."

"That's not my fault now, is it?"

"What's a fucking shipping investigator supposed to fucking do?"

"Collect information, find out when this wildcat strike's going to end so we can reschedule shipping accordingly."

For a moment it didn't appear that the man had understood. Glassy-eyed, he regarded Harry with baffled scrutiny. Then he blinked. Leaning over the bar he grasped hold of the morning paper and thrust it in Harry's face, so close he could scarcely be expected to read it. But he knew what it said. The Grand Jury had handed up a five-count indictment against Matt Braxton on charges of murder, assault, and conspiracy to commit murder. The trial, the story said, was likely to start soon given the enormous publicity surrounding the case. Defense attorneys were already saying that they would apply for change in venue, averring that their client could not hope to receive a fair trial in his home city. Actually, this promised to be only the first of at least two trials; he'd only been indicted for the slaying of Clay Meltzer and the attempts on Harry's life. He would then face charges in connection with the Tuber killings and have to go up on trial in Palo Alto.

But all these technical details did not interest the man speaking to Harry. The only thing that mattered to him was that his leader had been placed unceremoniously in the slammer and there was little likelihood that he'd be released soon.

"Fucking Bull," he was saying, no longer concerned what Harry did or did not do for a living. "He's telling us to go back to work. We'll fucking go back to work all right if they release Matt. If they don't, they better forget about it. We're shutting down the fucking docks. You tell your fucking shipping people they can get that through their fucking heads. You got that?"

Harry said he'd gotten it.

The man, however, didn't seem convinced he'd adequately made his point. "You think you've seen trouble you've seen nothing. You step over to Deringer's, well now I don't have to tell you, Mr. Investigator." He was turning coy. "You being what you say you are you should know these things."

What Harry knew was that Deringer's was a saloon favored by the union dissidents. Already there'd been some heated brawls there. But what he didn't know was what was planned—and when.

So Harry pretended not to be interested. "Nothing," he countered, "is going to happen over there. I've been there. Boring place you ask me."

"Oh you think so do you, Mr. Investigator? Tomorrow afternoon you be over there you see some fucking action."

The longshoreman was drunk and boastful and Harry didn't exactly invest him with much credibility. But the next afternoon he was there at Deringer's just in case Deringer's didn't really look very different than the bar habituated by Braxton's men; it was equally dark, and the air was stale and thick with the smell of booze that had spilled and had never been cleaned, and with the rancid stench of too many cigarettes lit up at once. The jukebox was filled with Irish music hall numbers, polkas, some C&W, none of it particularly to Harry's taste.

No one looked like they expected any trouble; either that or they'd grown so accustomed to it that they didn't bother making any special to-do over it. Every so often from down the other end of the bar you could hear a group of men arguing about the wildcat strike and the ultimate fate of Braxton and his disloyal successor, John Bull Ryan.

"Don't tell me he ain't got no influence down at City Hall," one was shouting, making himself heard over the din. "Hey, you read what it said in the papers today? Braxton's been transferred . . ."

Harry listened more intently; he had no idea what the man was referring to.

"What do you mean transferred?" another asked.

"He means just that. Read it myself." A third man was speaking now. "Braxton's been taken to a minimum security joint. Like those bastards from Watergate. Mitchell and Erlich-whatever his name was. Braxton's like them, he's got influence. TV all day long. Steak and lobster if he wants it. Living in clover. You and me did what he fuckin' did we'd be doing twenty-to-life in Soledad."

"That's the fuckin' truth," rejoindered the first one. "You watch, the guy'll be out on the streets again a couple of months, back in the fuckin' saddle. See what Bull does when that happens."

Harry was already at the pay phone, dialing the station.

He got Judson on the line. "What's this I hear about Braxton being transferred to minimum security?"

"I just heard about it like you, Harry. I swear no one told me a thing. In fact, no one here knew about it. We got the news from the radio."

"Who approved the transfer?"

"Beats me. Your guess is as good as mine."

Harry would have talked further, but just then he

noticed the appearance of three new men in the bar. They did not look like they belonged; one was distinguishable by the loss of more than half his nose; the other two didn't need any deformities to look menacing. All three were carrying beat-up canvas bags slung over their shoulders.

"Be with you later," Harry told Judson. "Have to get off now."

The three men took up position at the forward end of the bar; each ordered an ale. While they tried to be inconspicuous there was no way that this was going to be possible; furtively, they kept scanning the bar.

Harry had an idea that this trio could be counted on for an awful lot of trouble in the next few minutes or so. He was just about to fish another dime from his pocket and call the station again, this time to request backup, when four or five men crashed through the front door swinging clubs and bailing hooks. The three at the bar, right on cue, extracted their bailing hooks from the bags they were carrying and joined the fray.

With three men, Harry would have had hope of quelling the disturbance on his own. But with seven there was little likelihood of that—not when the antagonists and their victims were locked in such close combat; you fire on one you risked hitting the other.

The uproar was tremendous. Customers were collapsing with heads split open by pipes, the blood pouring in rivulets down their faces. One bulky longshoreman in a checkered flannel shirt was staggering towards the exit with a hook stuck half an inch or so into his back; he kept grasping for it, trying to get it out but for some reason he couldn't seem to locate it.

Harry turned back to the phone. No question he was going to need assistance; this was like a full scale riot only in strictly confined circumstances. But no sooner had he reached for the phone than the man with less than half a nose severed the cord connecting the receiver with his deftly wielded hook.

The assailant swept the hook up again, preparatory

to doing to Harry what he'd done to the cord. With no time to get out his weapon, Harry ducked his head and rammed it directly into Half-nose's abdomen, sending him reeling back a couple of feet. And a couple of feet was all he could go since the place was so packed. But he still had a steady grip on the hook and there was no question he'd had years of experience using it, though not always on other human beings. He lunged again, driving the sharp end of the instrument toward Harry's left side. Shifting to the right and taking a step backward, Harry managed to avoid the worst of the blow. Still the hook did connect, tearing through the bottom part of his jacket and then through his shirt and into his skin. The wound wasn't serious but it produced a good deal of blood which seemed to renew Half-nose's enthusiasm. With a sort of banshee wail, he went in for the attack again, ready to drive the hook home straight into Harry's chest.

Harry caught hold of his arm before he could complete the motion necessary to sink the hook into him while at the same time delivering a ruthless punch into his solar plexus, just about knocking the wind wholly out of him. The impact of Harry's blow had the effect of causing Half-nose to weaken his grip on the hook though he still struggled to retain hold of it.

As Harry sought to close him out with another strong punch, Half-nose's friend—the one with a yellow Addidas T-shirt—had slipped up behind him with his bailing hook. The rounded end of the hook was stained with blood nearly up to the handle.

Addidas, a savage look to his face, brought the hook back so that it would have the full force of his weight when it struck Harry. But there was so little room to execute the maneuver that this proved impossible. Two men were battling it out right in back of him—one with fists, the other with a rattling chain that he kept slamming against his enemy's ribs—and so Addidas was propelled up almost directly against Harry.

Harry, sensing his presence, shifted, but because he was still concentrating on Half-nose, he could not take sufficient precautions to avoid Addidas' assault altogether. The sudden sting in the back of his shoulder jolted him. He turned so suddenly that Addidas had not yet had a chance to extract the hook. Half-nose meanwhile was still doubled up and retching from the blows Harry had inficted on him.

Ignoring the weapon that protruded awkwardly from his back, releasing a thin line of blood that would have been greater had the hook not been staunching the wound, Harry confronted Addidas. And because Addidas now lacked any weapon aside from his hands, Harry had the advantage.

But it was an advantage that was quickly fading. Like the earlier injury between his ribs, the wound the hook had produced directly under the shoulder blade was not very serious, but still it had the effect of numbing an ever widening area, making it more and more difficult for him to use his right arm. No matter, his left was good enough for the task at hand. He gained hold of his .44 and was on the verge of removing it when Addidas saw his chance and went in at Harry, hoping to take him off guard. Despite his wounds, Harry was more nimble than he'd suspected and with his right leg delivered a lethal straight kick that threw Addidas back, sending him sprawling right into the two combatants struggling to the rear of him. He surprised one of his allies who ended up inadvertently slashing him in the face with the chain. First an ugly elongated gash appeared running across his face at an angle—from his brow to nearly his jaw—and then it opened, erupting with so much blood that it obscured the left side of his face. He was stunned all right, but still functional.

Half-nose, however, had managed to gain a vertical posture and was beginning to renew his assault on Harry. The assault got nowhere. Harry, tiring from the wounds, was in no mood to continue struggling with him. In a gesture that Half-nose somehow missed in all the confusion, Harry brought the barrel of the .44 hard down on his head, knocking him out cold. With this motion, the hook slipped out of his back.

Turning his attention now to the conflicts raging in other parts of the bar, Harry realized that Braxton's shock troops, having the advantage of surprise and being more heavily armed, were getting the best of it.

He had no time to reflect on the situation. One man who'd dropped out of the fight early—clubbed into submission by the bartender who could clobber someone with a bottle of B&B as well as he could pour it—began to show signs of life again. Shaking himself free from his daze, he needed a moment to orient himself. That done, he raised himself to full height—and full height came near to seven feet—and searched for some object suitable enough to reduce a man to a protracted state of unconsciousness. Almost obliviously, he began picking out glass splinters from the B&B bottle that were strewn about his hair. At last his reddened eyes hit upon a harpoon that was suspended above the tarnished mirror behind the bar. The harpoon probably went back to the eighteenth century during the heyday of the whaling industry. Not that Sleeping Beauty cared about its venerable history. He just wanted to participate in the fight before it ended, regretting that he'd been senseless throughout most of it. So, groaning with effort, he extended his arms up over the bar and seized hold of the harpoon. Tugging at it with his powerful arms, he succeeded in getting it down.

Delighted with this accomplishment, Sleeping Beauty turned and rushed Harry—Harry being the most available target at the time—the rusted point of the weapon aimed directly at his chest. Harry failed to observe him, for he was too preoccupied with Addidas. Bloody and hurt as he was, Addidas seemed intent on inflicting further injury on Harry. Somehow he'd come up with a new weapon, a tire chain this time, and he was lashing it through the air, creating an unimpeded path for him in Harry's direction. He appeared not to notice the .44 in Harry's hand, an unforgivable oversight.

Harry allowed Addidas to approach him, ducking to avoid the chain, then fired one round into Addidas' kneecap. The kneecap exploded and Addidas was pivoted right around and fell, screaming to the ground. At that moment, out of the corner of his eye, Harry saw not Sleeping Beauty but the tip of the hundred-year-old harpoon. He had no idea what it was, he couldn't get a clear glimpse of it, but he had the foresight to jump clear of it, simultaneously going into a crouch and letting off two additional rounds, both of which took Sleeping Beauty, once in his upper chest, above his heart, the other in the neck which entered at such a decided angle that it continued to travel up through his throat and into his brain where it must have stopped somewhere because certainly it didn't emerge. Sleeping Beauty's eyes clouded and almost immediately began filling up with blood hemorrhaging inside the occipital lobe. He was not alive and yet he continued to remain upright for another few seconds before collapsing in a heap, his hand still clutching the ornamental harpoon. Sleeping Beauty was going to be sleeping forever.

Whether it was his death, and the sudden realization that the battle had escalated beyond the use of bottles, clubs, hooks, and chains, or whether there was some prearranged signal given, Harry could not be certain. In any case, all at once, the bloodied but more or less victorious remnants of Braxton's troops disengaged themselves and made for the exit.

A few men, who still had their skulls and bodies intact, pursued them outside but there was little point in it. A delivery truck was waiting directly in front of Deringer's and the escaping dock workers simply piled into it. Before anyone had a chance to stop them, the truck had pulled away from the curb and was heading fast toward Jefferson.

Only then did Harry hear, but still way in the distance, the familiar whine of police sirens. It seemed reasonable to have expected them before this. Even though Harry himself had not had the opportunity to call for backup surely the commotion in the bar was loud enough to have alerted anyone in the vicinity to the fact that something more than a common tavern brawl was in progress inside.

Once again Harry was confirmed in his judgment that someone—and someone very high up in the administration—was directing things on behalf of Braxton, deliberately delaying police reinforcements and sabotaging all efforts to settle the wildcat walkout peacefully. And Harry knew also that should he discover who it was he would be in far deeper trouble than he was now.

But at this juncture he could scarcely be bothered thinking about any of that. His wounds needed tending to and he had to go home and get a good long sleep. Not as long as Sleeping Beauty's, but long.

Fourteen

There was no way for Harry to sleep. Despite the care that the doctor had lavished on him, stitching back the torn skin and the underlying strata of muscles, the pain could be awakened at any time just by applying the smallest bit of pressure to the bandaged wounds. On his back or on his side, these injuries reasserted themselves. Even when at last he could contort himself into a position that did not hurt him, he would usually make the mistake of rolling over in his sleep and sleep would end right there; he'd regain consciousness with a groan and a hatred of the antagonists who'd given him this pain that went beyond what animosity he'd felt when he was actually trying to subdue them.

So it was that at quarter past three in the morning, five days after the incident at Deringer's, Harry was still awake, having resigned himself to another sleepless night. The doctor had given him a prescription to alleviate the pain, but Harry chose not to take it. He was not sure himself why not but thus far he'd made it on coffee and a few medicinal shots of whiskey and that was quite sufficient.

At three in the morning when the phone rings it's either a wrong number or bad news. Very seldom is it anything else. Which was why Harry stared long and hard at the phone before he answered it.

132

"Callahan."

"Harry Callahan?"

He recognized the woman's voice. The same informant who'd phoned him the last time about the plans Lesko and Passaretti had to kill him. She was a woman with a lot of credibility, whoever she was.

"That's right. Who is this?" He knew she wouldn't tell him but figured he'd try anyway.

"There's no need for you to know that. Look, I can't talk long. You know where they've taken Braxton to?"

"I've heard."

"Then you'll want to know that at two-fifteen tomorrow morning he'll be sprung." She waited for a reaction. "You hear me?"

"Yes, I did."

"That gives you less than twenty-four hours. You'll have to act pretty damn quick." With that she hung up.

This information tended not to surprise Harry. He didn't doubt what this unidentified woman said for one minute. Whoever it was watching over Braxton had obviously concluded that he might actually end up losing his case and be convicted. Better then to engineer his escape. What mystified Harry was what this woman's involvement with Braxton's organization was and why she was so anxious to screw him.

What Harry should have done, what he was fully expected to do, was to inform Bressler of what he'd learned and let him deal with it. But Harry was never one for going through proper channels in any case; and in this instance, it was too risky. Bressler might forward the information all right but somewhere along the line it would get stonewalled. Even to go directly to the prison authorities would be a mistake; Harry assumed that someone in the chief warden's office would probably have been compromised, too.

Since these alternatives were pretty much foreclosed to him, he realized he would have to once again work on his own. In fact, he wasn't even supposed to report back to duty until the following Monday; he'd been given time off to recuperate adequately from the wounds he'd sustained at Deringer's.

Well, it wouldn't be the first time he put himself on the line with no expectation of assistance from his own department.

It was one of those cold drizzly San Francisco nights that look lovely and romantic when they're put on film but in actuality, leave something to be desired. The dampness in the air was insidious; fifteen minutes of being exposed to it and you were chilled to the marrow.

The way this particular minimum-security institution was designed reflected the ease with which someone could escape from it. For one thing, the northern extension of it ran parallel to part of Golden Gate Park; it wouldn't be difficult for someone to lose himself in the brambles of a thickly wooded area there. It seemed the most likely site for a prospective escape Harry had concluded after having made a surreptitious surveillance that afternoon. However, it now appeared to him that the escape was to occur on the opposite side, adjoining the street.

The gray-blue limousine that was parked immediately below the prison wall, with its motor running and its headlights doused, provided Harry with all the evidence he needed. It was scarcely past two and the fine drizzle that had been coming down ever since nightfall had begun to turn into a fog that all but obscured the low-lying wall over which Harry expected Braxton to come.

Across the street Harry remained in his car, alternately fixing his eyes on the limo and on the wall. As far as he could tell, the fog and the darkness together shielded him from view.

But as it drew close to fifteen minutes past the hour Harry slipped out of the car and quietly made his way down the street, approaching nearer to the prison. He still was scrupulous about keeping silent: just another shadow loose in the damp.

Two minutes to go—if what the woman had told him was correct. Two minutes and yet there was no sign of any activity along the walls. From time to time a searchlight slashed the fog but it illuminated next to nothing. This being a minimum-security institution, there wasn't an abundance of guards to begin with and in this particular quadrant there were, as far as Harry could see, none at all.

Braxton was late—by five minutes—but he came. Harry was not disappointed. At first he could hardly be sure there was anyone moving along the wall, so dense was the fog. But little by little a figure, diminutive-looking from such a distance, emerged from the murk. A rope was flung down and it reached to about two feet above the ground. The wall itself must not have been any higher than fifteen feet.

Although he'd gotten on in years and was not in the best of shape, Braxton still displayed an enviable dexterity as he negotiated his way down the rope. He wasn't slow by any means and he betrayed no sense of panic; apparently he was certain that no one would interfere with his progress.

Harry waited until Braxton had his feet on the ground before he advanced toward him, gun in hand. As hard as he was concentrating on Braxton he kept one eye on the Lincoln which now was pulling up in their direction. The Lincoln's headlights suddenly went on, throwing the two of them into relief. Braxton blinked, for the first time sighting Harry. He blinked again, caught between bolting for the vehicle that was about to carry him away and remaining absolutely still lest Harry blow him into another and not necessarily better world.

"Mr. Braxton, I suggest you hold up right there."

In desperation Braxton gazed toward the limousine; between the fog and the intense glare from the headlights it was impossible to make out just who the occupants of the vehicle were.

No sooner had Harry gotten the words out of his

135

mouth than he became aware of a car coming up in back of him. The roar that its motor produced was monstrously loud, its tires screamed against the pavement.

Automatically, Harry turned just in time to see the front of an Impala, gleaming chrome, materializing from out of the thickening fog. Having shot around the corner, it was now bearing right down on Harry, leaving him only seconds in which to act before being pinned to the prison wall and quite possibly crushed into that very wall.

He leapt to the left and as far as he could to avoid the Impala but in doing so he stumbled, half-falling. The Impala at the last moment skillfully maneuvered itself off the sidewalk and back out onto the street again. Harry, still in an awkward position, let loose three rounds at the departing car but he was deprived of the satisfaction of seeing any of them do damage.

Of course, Braxton was nowhere to be seen. While Harry was busy saving his ass, Braxton's friends had snatched him away. It was hardly much of a surprise.

Fifteen

Braxton had arranged his escape too late for it to make the early editions of the papers but the wire services and radio news commentators were not subject to the constraints of such deadlines. Outrage was the one word that described reaction the best. Authorities, all sorts of authorities—the mayor (through his press secretary), the police commissioner, the correctional system's administrator, the chief warden of the prison itself—all vowed to undertake prompt investigations into the escape of Matt Braxton. Naturally, no one admitted guilt or complicity but rather expressed astonishment that such a thing could have happened. Opinion was divided among the public— at least that part of the public which was randomly sampled by reporters; half of them believed that Braxton's escape proved that he must have been guilty, the other half thought that he had no other choice but to escape since he was bound to be framed and convicted.

In situations like this Harry knew what happened was that a scapegoat—probably some poor sucker who worked as a guard—would be quickly found, tried, and punished, just so that the whole affair could be gotten off the front pages and expunged from the public's memory which was scarcely a problem, the public's memory being notoriously short. And Braxton would still be at large, living not like a fugitive afraid of every shadow but rather as an exiled potentate who'd not neglected to take the national treasury with him when he fled his native land.

Only one benefit seemed to have resulted from the escape, if the news commentators were to be believed (and they weren't, Harry was convinced) and that was that the picket lines were beginning to come down on the docks and the men, who'd gone off the job illegally, were returning to work. What no one seemed to realize was that this was the price exacted for abetting Braxton's bid for freedom. It was to Harry an obvious *quid pro quo;* you scatch my back, I'll scratch yours.

It wasn't the lingering pain from his wounds nor the depleted condition of his body from getting too little sleep but rather an overwhelming sense of futility that wearied Harry. You work your ass off, you struggle mightily to do your job, only to have someone snatch the rug right out from under you. He felt at that moment that he would have done better to be giving out speeding tickets. At least he would have half a chance of actually apprehending an offender without someone interferring all the time.

Toward evening he decided that he would take a therapeutic walk and set out from his apartment building in no particular direction.

It wasn't long, however, before he realized that he was being followed. There was a car—a cream-colored Seville—tailing him half a block behind and on the other side of the street. It crept along for a while, then stopped. Harry kept going but he maintained a leisurely pace, interested to see who it was. He doubted that it was a professional. No professional would be so clumsy and obvious in his surveillance.

Harry turned a corner and, pressing himself into a doorway out of sight, waited for the tail to catch up.

It sure wasn't what he'd expected. A tall, leggy woman who'd probably long ago forgotten what color her hair used to be. She had come to a halt, astonished and a bit irritated to discover that her quarry had vanished. She put a finger under her lip as a sign of puzzlement and turned in place, looking every which way for Harry. Because she did not expect to see Harry concealed in the shadows of the doorway, she failed to find him.

Instead, Harry made himself known to her, coming up right in back of her and taking her by surprise. She let out a stifled scream and pressed her hand to her heart. "Oh," she said, "you frightened me!"

The voice; Harry identified it immediately. It was the voice of the woman who'd called him twice before.

"You were looking for me?"

"Well, no, actually . . . Why should I be looking for you?"

Harry shrugged. "I don't know. These days a lot of people look for me, it's contagious." He started to walk away from her.

"Wait a minute. I'm sorry, yes, I was looking for you. I don't know why I said that just now."

Harry turned to look at her. Not bad looking, he considered, but she had an unhealthy neurotic energy to her which was obvious simply by the hunger in her eyes and the excessiveness of her gestures; it was not enough for her to exhibit her emotions on her face, her whole body was marshaled to dramatize them.

"You have a name?"

"Well, yes . . ." Even at this late date she was reluctant to divulge it. "Andrea Foley."

"Now tell me what your real name is."

Because she'd been helpful to him twice before Harry resisted the impulse to express his impatience. He had the feeling that he was going to have to coax even the most trivial bit of information from her now that she had finally decided to appear in person.

"Darlene Farley," she said. It was as though she were apologizing. "I don't know where I got Andrea Foley from. It just came to me on the spur of the moment." She kept her eyes away from Harry; clearly she was embarrassed.

"I expect you might have something to say to me."

"I guess I do."

"All right then. There's a place we can talk in privacy."

If Darlene Farley had anticipated an intimate atmosphere for their conversation she was sure to be disappointed. A place called Kwik-Lunch was hardly the setting for an exchange of confidences. On the other hand, Harry was comfortable in this pedestrian hamburger establishment and never had to worry about being disrupted at his meals, such as they were.

"The usual, Mr. Callahan?" Jaffee, the proprietor, called from behind the counter. As soon as Harry signaled that he was in no mood to try anything new, he was already throwing a meat patty on the grill. "And for you, Miss?"

"Just a cup of coffee."

They took a seat at a table some distance from the window.

There was a moment of silence. Darlene was evidently waiting for Harry to speak but he had settled back to let her do all the talking.

At last she said, "You let him get away."

"I did what I could. Some things I can't control."

She did not seem to hear what he said. "You shouldn't have let him escape. Now you'll never get him back inside."

"What's Matt Braxton to you?"

"Do I have to tell you?"

"This is no court of law, lady, so if you'd rather not tell me don't. But I hate having my time wasted."

She picked up a cigarette and tried lighting it with one of those gold lighters that look fine but don't operate the way they should. The flame flickered erratically and she had to repeatedly fiddle with it before she was satisfied. "We're lovers. That is, we used to be. He's a son of a bitch, a real bastard."

"I kind of got that impression myself."

"He's fucking around, but he expects me to remain

140

faithful. He has these eunuchs—well, they're not really eunuchs but they might as well be—they're supposed to look out for me." At this her eyes went to the window. "I don't know whether they suspect me yet. But he's still got people following me. Only reason nothing's happened so far is he thinks me too dumb a broad to worry about. The way he figures it, no one crosses Matt Braxton. No one's even clever enough to cut him down. Maybe that's why I'm doing it, to prove he's wrong. Am I making any sense?"

"I think so." He recalled the old saying about a woman scorned and the fury she could ignite that hell couldn't match. Well, there was some truth to the adage.

"If I told you where he's gone would you be able to do something about it?"

"Depends what you mean by doing something."

"Look, one of these days he's going to find out what I've done. I told you so far I'm all right. But sooner or later Matt'll find out and then I'm fucked. There's no other way to put it, I'm afraid." In her distractedness she had difficulty concentrating on what she was saying; her gaze was constantly directed on the street or that portion of it that the front window of Kwik-Lunch revealed. "I shouldn't have taken the Seville. It's too easy to spot," she remarked.

Harry tried bringing her back to the subject at hand. "Where is he?"

"Tapaquite," she answered right away.

"Where the hell's that?"

"Lesser Antilles, oh, a little south of St. Lucia and St. Vincent but north of Grenada. It's not much of an island but there's a thriving tourist business there. I know. Matt took me there a few times. Always business trips, tax deductible. He owns half the island. I don't know, maybe he owns the whole thing. I wouldn't be surprised. Where do you think all that money he's been ripping off from the union pension funds has been going all these years?" She looked triumphantly at Harry, then went on.

"He's been investing in hotels and casinos. Not alone, of course. The Syndicate's sharing expenses. I don't know to what extent but they're involved. They've always been involved."

"Ah, so that's where the Chicago boys come in."

"What?"

"Nothing. Go on."

"So he's down there. They had a plane waiting for him last night. It took him right there. Of course, it's hopeless to try to get him back with what do they call it?"

"Extradition proceedings?"

"Extradition proceedings, that's it. He owns the island, he owns the government. Just a bunch of spades anyway. His word's law down there. Hell, it's law up here, too, isn't it? Every fucking where he goes it's the same story."

"I see," was all that Harry would say.

"So what are you planning to do?"

"I don't know yet."

"Well, I wish you'd do something fast."

Harry gave her a wan smile. "You can be sure, Miss Farley, that whatever I decide to do it'll be fast."

Harry didn't wait until Monday to return to the department. He showed up late that same afternoon. Bressler was surprised to see him and not what you'd call exactly pleased. But then again he was never very pleased to see Harry.

"What's the matter, Harry? Couldn't stay away from work, you had to come back for the weekend?"

"I'd like to put in a request for a vacation."

Bressler didn't frown precisely but he did something with his jaw muscles that approximated a frown.

"A vacation, you say? Take a little time off from duty and you get to enjoying the easy life, is that it?"

In no mood to argue, Harry didn't respond.

"How long would you be going for?"

"A week. Make it a week and a half. Ten days."

"OK, tell you what you do. Fill out the forms and get them to me. At this point I don't see any reason why your request should be denied. Now that this shit on the docks is settled we got a little room to breathe. Harry?"

"What is it?"

"This vacation, where would you be going?"

"The Caribbean."

Bressler nodded. "Nice place, the Caribbean, especially this season. But I got to tell you, I wouldn't figure you for lying on a beach collecting a tan."

"Everyone needs a change."

"Yeah," Bressler said as if this were a revelation for him, "I suppose they do."

Sixteen

From San Juan Harry caught an Air France plane south to Fort-de-France on Martinique. There he was obliged to wait for four hours for a shuttle to Ocho Rios on Tapaquite. This shuttle was an antiquated Cessna that had seen much better days; it remained aloft only with reluctance, at the mercy of winds that buffeted it about, while below the glistening blue-green waters of the Caribbean remained lovingly tranquil, stirred up only by the occasional fast-moving power boat.

The only other people on board this shaky craft—and there weren't more than a dozen in all—looked like their purpose in going to Tapaquite was probably not very legitimate. They all bore the appearance of millionaires who having derived their fortunes from shady enterprises had salted the whole lot of it away and were now resolved to indulge themselves with all that untaxed wealth. Their skin was either too white or else floridly red from too sudden an exposure to the tropical sun and their bellies protruded like pregnant women's. Which was another thing that Harry noticed; only two women were on board—and one of them was the lone stewardess, whose insolent stare caused passengers to think twice before making any requests of her. The other woman was apparently the wife of the Hispanic man sitting next to her; she wasn't attractive and the husband seemed completely bored with her, preferring to stare out the oval window at the sea than give her the time of day.

Harry had taken the precaution of disguising himself, not wishing to alert Braxton or his henchmen to his presence on the island, not immediately anyway. He'd chosen the same costume he'd worn when meeting with the hitmen Longlegs had introduced him to that afternoon on Fishermen's Wharf: wig, loud shirt, white ducks. He could have passed as an ambitious entrepreneur, maybe a gun smuggler and or high-priced consultant promoting Caribbean real estate or tax shelter deals on the Cayman Islands, someone who was out to make a killing. Well, that was true in a sense; he was out to make a killing.

The Cessna landed like it flew, with uncertainty. The bump the wheels made on the asphalt surface of the airstrip caused the seats to wobble as though they were soon to pop out of their moorings. The dozen passengers seemed to breathe a collective sigh of relief once it was clear that the plane was down, and down to stay.

The airport at Ocho Rios—which was all that the island had to offer in the way of a capital—was a modest affair: two airstrips, neither of them large enough to accomodate a craft larger than the Cessna, and a brand new terminal that appeared to be constructed without the benefit of an architect's planning; cement ladled over glass.

One customs inspector was all that they had, but then there wasn't much use for another. There was only one flight into Ocho Rios a day—and that was only in good weather.

This inspector barely glanced at either Harry or at his passport (which like his disguise revealed another identity: James A. Balsam, born in Seattle, Washington). As soon as he was out in the central terminal area he was besieged by a small army of boys and aged men with coconut skins who offered to carry his bags and transport him into the city proper which was a distance of ten miles away. Harry selected one man who could have been thirty or sixty-five, whose face was shadowed by a wide-rimmed straw hat. Despite Harry's protest, he insisted on grasping hold of his one bag and lugging it out to his cab.

The cab, a dented, obsolete green Ford, circa 1950, looked like it wasn't going to make it farther than the next block. The windshield was cracked into a web that made viewing through it virtually impossible.

It lumbered and lurched and rattled, this cab, but the damn thing moved, inching laboriously up the hilly road, stirring up a cloud of dust as it went. All the while the driver rambled on, mixing the local patois with a strange brand of English so Harry couldn't make heads or tails out of what he was saying, though he did gather that he was recommending one hotel in town over the other, no doubt because his preferred hotel gave him a commission for each new guest he brought in.

At a sharp bend in the unpaved road, the driver stopped abruptly, gesturing out to Harry's right. There was a wide stretch of tangled growth, broken here and there by mimosa and palms whose fronds extended almost to blot out the dazzling late afternoon sun; beyond that you couldn't see much at all. Harry couldn't understand what it was that so sparked the driver's interest. All he could make out were the words—"Boca de la Sierpe" —which he repeated incessantly.

"What's there? What should I know about Boca de la Sierpe?"

"Grande casa," the driver said. "Grande casa de Senor Braxton."

He didn't pronounce Braxton correctly but there was no doubting whom he was referring to. Somewhere through the undergrowth then was Braxton's home-away-from-home. Obviously if this underpaid taxi driver was aware of where Braxton was living then so was everyone else on the island.

"You bring many people here?"

The driver couldn't comprehend him. Harry did his best to make himself clear but further communication was out of the question. The driver resumed his erratic progress into Ocho Rios.

Tapaquite's capital was like an Old West town waiting for the gold rush to get to it; there was a Crown Street, a Prince Street, and a Kingston Street, all testifying to a colonial British heritage. Where the three collided a vast square—Plaza de Armas—formed and it was here in this square that all the business, cultural and political life of the city was conducted. Opposite the sprawling porticoed capital building was the Whitby Hotel, a white stucco structure with all its windows shuttered against the intense heat. It was either the Whitby or the Crown Bay which could be found, as its name implied, closer to the shore. The driver advocated the Whitby; Harry took one look at it and decided on the Crown Bay. More inconspicuous, he reasoned. The driver complained furiously but at length relented.

The room given Harry was small and dense with moisture that had seeped in from the bay. Particles of salt had encrusted on the small bureau which, aside from the bed and one chair, was the only piece of furniture in the place. There was one amenity and that was a small balcony that adjoined the room. Harry walked out onto it.

From where he stood, leaning against the rusted railing, he could see the jetty to which three sailboats and several motor launches were tied. Boys were running barefoot from one craft to the next, performing a variety of tasks to ensure that everything was seaworthy.

Now another boat, a sleek fiberglass model—a forty-footer it looked like from this distance—appeared on the horizon and with a sudden slowing of its motors, circled in toward the shore.

Harry watched as it docked and as its passengers, one by one, climbed out onto the jetty. There were a couple of splendid-looking women, gloriously tanned, the sort you see in magazine ads for cosmetics, toiletries, and cigarettes, full of the promise of romance in exchange for the purchase of some commodity or other.

But as arresting as these women were, it was the men that provoked Harry's interest. Though they had come into port on a pleasure craft and though they were casually attired, in T-shirts, shorts, and sneakers, there was an air of enforced jollity about them. They were not men who could relax easily. Underneath their light jackets and secreted in the canvas bags they carried Harry was sure there were sidearms. He assumed that at any moment Braxton would be stepping out onto the jetty. Another man might remain secluded, fearful of exposure in light of the fact that he was being sought for murder and escape. But not Matt Braxton. For him, hiding would be an admission of cowardice and that was something even the bitterest opponent of the union president had never accused him of.

And sure enough, after another minute or two had passed, Braxton emerged from below deck, one arm lazily curled about the waist of a slender brunette who was in the process of adjusting her bikini top. Except for the color of her hair she could have passed as a duplicate of Darlene Farley.

His retinue protectively surrounding him, Braxton, with a sprightly step, started down the length of the jetty. Harry decided to see just where it was he was headed.

It did not take long to find out; Braxton and his crew had seated themselves in the Leeward Cay, a restaurant-cafe that looked out onto the shimmering water.

Harry, unobserved by anyone in Braxton's party, took an inconspicuous position at the bar. There the bartender, a corpulent very swarthy man who hailed from Queens, of all places, told Harry that Braxton and his companions arrived every day at the Cay, and always at the same time: half-past five. Sometimes they would linger on for dinner or go up to the Whitby or else they would go back to Boca de la Sierpe. "He's getting so bored with this ginmill," the bartender said, "that he's thinking of building another just so he'll have somewhere new to go to."

148

"And that's what he does with his time?"

"Well, he's still busy running his scams Stateside I hear. See that fellow over there? The one in the turtleneck with the earring in his ear? He's new. Every afternoon it's someone new. He comes in on the shuttle and soon as he turns up at Boca Braxton takes him out for a sail. I figure he's given a broad for his trouble, too. They discuss a little business, then a day or two later, the guy flies out again."

Harry recognized the man from the plane but made no acknowledgment of this.

The bartender was probably used to getting no response from his customers; he was a regular gossipmonger. "They say Braxton's still pulling the strings up California way. These jokers who come in, they're nothing but errand boys. Well-paid, but an errand boy's an errand boy. Ask anyone."

"What happens here at night?" Harry asked.

"Place called the Serendip. Another called the Mimoso. Both of them just installed discotheques to go with the casinos. It's either one or the other. This ginmill, we close up half-past ten. Braxton and his crew will usually put in at the Serendip. Costs more. I don't think old Matt likes the place, but these broads he's got with and all these people coming down from the States, they're looking for action. You know how it is?"

Harry had an idea how it was, and that evening he followed the Braxton party into the Serendip. It was a brightly lit, festively colored nightspot: lots of pretty women with necklines scooped halfway to their navels and obsequious waiters looking very uncomfortable in stiff red uniforms. There was a choice of losing your money at roulette, blackjack, or at the one-armed bandits. Drinks, invariably ingenious rum concoctions, cost what a native of Tapaquite made in a week. Only two couples occupied the small circular dance floor.

Twenty minutes had elapsed since Harry had entered the Serendip and now two men, one white, one black, approached the bar. Where they'd come from was hard to

149

say. One minute they weren't there, the next they were. With deceptive casualness they moved in on either side of Harry.

"Mr. Balsam," the white began, "are you enjoying our little island?"

"We don't usually get too many tourists this time of year," the black added, flashing a smile.

"My travel agent doesn't know any better," Harry offered, all the while scanning the length of the room. While neither Braxton nor any of those with him seemed remotely interested in him, there were others, scattered at various tables, who had their eyes fixed on him. Even a few of the red-jacketed waiters, with their impassive and unreadable expressions, now appeared strangely menacing. It was very likely that no one would come to Harry's aid if a fight broke out.

Under such circumstances it was always best, Harry knew, to take preemptive action, get a jump on the situation before the advantage totally slipped from one's grasp.

"So tell us, Mr. Balsam, what does bring you to Tapaquite?" the white asked, clearly not caring what his answer would be.

"I like a place where the natives are friendly," Harry replied, then took a step away from the bar. "Excuse me, gentlemen."

The black gripped hold of one arm, the white of the other.

"Not going so soon?" said the black.

"And we were just getting to know one another," his companion put in.

"Yeah, it's a damn shame, isn't it?"

The two men were trying to steer Harry out of the bar without attracting attention.

Harry allowed them to take him toward the exit, luring them into thinking they were in control. He then held back half a step and with expert skill, slid his right leg between the white's, curling it sharply and hard around his left so as to knock him off-balance. As the white lurched forward, his hold on Harry loosened sufficiently for Harry to free his arm. Then with his elbow he struck out against the man's back, propelling him forward. In the few seconds that it took to execute this attack, the man on Harry's other side began to turn. But he was unprepared for Harry's assault. No sooner had he tripped the white than Harry threw his entire weight behind a right hook directed at the black. The black dodged it but in doing so surrendered his hold on Harry's arm.

Harry then brought up his left knee, smacking it ruthlessly into the black's stomach, pitching him backward with such momentum that he landed clumsily on the tiled floor. The sound his skull made against the hard surface was ominously loud. By this time the white had recovered enough to face Harry again, this time with an elongated aluminum instrument in his hands. As Harry advanced toward him, the man, to his great surprise, drew the instrument up to his lips and aimed it at his chest. A blowgun. The last thing that Harry had expected. Such was his astonishment that he hardly had time to get out of the way of the steel dart.

The dart was four inches in length and had the capacity to penetrate through half an inch of plywood. There being no plywood in the vicinity, it thunked straight into the oaken panel of the bar directly behind Harry. Already a second dart had been thrust into the gun, preparatory to launch. The man was good; you had to give him that much. He was fast and good. It occurred to Harry that the tips of the steel darts might be doused with some kind of drug, maybe with what they used to stun elephants and tigers.

When the second dart came toward him he simply ducked, scraping the floor with his knees. The dart continued on, catching by sheer accident the black who was just getting to his feet again. The dart hit him in his arm. He emitted a cry of pain, lurched crazily, and collapsed to

151

the floor with more finality than he had the first time, confirming Harry's guess that the darts were contaminated.

Stepping back, the white was in the process of reloading his weapon, evidently unconcerned that his comrade had become unwittingly his victim in place of Harry.

Harry ran headlong into him, like a linebacker for the Steelers, forcing him down. The dart gun got flung aside in the confusion, but the white still held onto one of the darts with which he attempted to stab Harry. Lunging out, he used the dart like a short dagger, indifferent as to where he cut Harry because it really didn't matter so long as he could open skin and send the drug rushing into Harry's bloodstream.

Harry heard his sleeve rip but the dart failed to penetrate any deeper; the man beneath him simply hadn't the purchase necessary to drive it home with any force. Harry leapt up suddenly, but before his antagonist could take advantage of his unexpected freedom, Harry sent his heel down hard against the man's right hand which contained the dart. The blow was of sufficient strength and his hand had been so positioned that Harry succeeded in breaking three of his fingers. The bones cracked audibly and were then slowly ground into a consistency that resembled a fine dust. The man's face contorted with pain, and he shrieked loud enough to awaken all the dead of Tapaquite—and with Braxton's presence on the island there were sure to be a lot of them.

The intensity of pain that shot up from his crushed hand was so great, in fact, that the white could concentrate on nothing else. Rather than try to get up and resume the confrontation, he merely released a hapless sigh, rolled over, and began to vomit.

It was only now that Harry had a chance to see how the Serendip's clientele and staff had reacted to this unscheduled show. Not surprisingly, all eyes were focused on him. A pall of silence—but expectant silence all the same—had fallen over the room and even the ongoing blare of disco music could scarcely intrude upon it. The people who were giving him the most concerted stares were those who sat at Braxton's table. But far from appearing distressed that their boys had come through this engagement so poorly they looked almost—well, pleased. Particularly Braxton. He was smiling. At first, Harry thought that his eyes had deceived him. Braxton smiling? Whatever for? He couldn't possibly imagine.

Of course, they knew his identity. They might have known it ever since he got on the plane at Fort-de-France in Martinique. Then why should they resemble delighted children at Barnum & Bailey's Circus?

At any rate, the Serendip's management was not at all happy about this disruption. Bad for the Serendip's reputation. The waiters though moved with incredible speed in removing the two luckless henchmen, both of whom were groaning at different volumes.

Those waiters who were not involved in the clean-up of bodies and vomit were now, at a respectable distance, forming a circle around Harry. An astonishing amount of hardware was suddenly produced from underneath their red jackets, small black handguns, nothing showy but effective nonetheless. Maybe, Harry thought, they were used to this sort of thing.

Harry saw the futility of resisting. He did not think that he would be shot right here, in full view of the clientele, even if Braxton supporters and hangers-on were in abundance. But being shot somewhere where it was dark, the alleyway outside, didn't quite appeal to Harry either.

"I think, sir," said the maitre d', "I think you would be advised to go home and to make it a point not to return to the Serendip in the future."

A reasonable man, Harry thought, all things considered.

"My sentiments exactly," Harry said. Then, without looking back, he strolled to the door, not absolutely certain that one of these pistol-wielding waiters might not decide to shoot him just for the hell of it.

Now that his cover was blown Harry recognized the futility of his disguise and immediately dispensed with the wig which was, with the heavy island heat, pretty uncomfortable in any case. He ditched it in the bay and watched it sail languidly out to sea.

He figured it this way; if Braxton knows I'm here I might as well turn up every place he goes, haunt him like the ghost of Bernie Tuber; but he had to give Braxton the impression that it was not only he—Harry Callahan—stalking him but that he had backup assistance, undercover agents ready to jump in should he come to any harm. If Braxton was convinced he was acting alone, why then he would have no compunction about blowing him away and sending him floating after the wig he'd worn for the better part of the preceding day. Tomorrow, he promised himself, he would scatter some cash about Ocho Rios's unemployed, pay them to dog Braxton's footsteps, put some fear into him. Not too much fear though; Harry didn't want Braxton pulling out and setting himself up on some other unfortunate Caribbean island. If that happened he'd have to start all over again.

The lobby of the Crown Bay was deader than the parched, browning fronds of the potted palms that were set in its corners. The man at the desk had fallen asleep his head buried in the middle of the huge black, half-empty register. A clock ticked noisily behind him indicating a time separated from the correct time by several hours. A bloated but very colorful waterbug of some sort traipsed across Harry's path, undoubtedly on his way to join his family burrowed in the crumbling plaster walls.

Harry's room was located on the third floor. The light grew dimmer and dimmer the higher you got. Either the bulbs had burned out and had not been replaced or else the sockets were empty, gaping holes that in the dark looked like open wounds.

In his flight down to the Caribbean Harry had not lost that sixth sense of his that warned him when something was not as it should be. Approaching his room, he muffled his footsteps, then stepping up to the door he pu

154

his ear to it and listened. He could hear nothing. But he was convinced that in his absence his room had been invaded.

Quietly he inserted his key in the door. Still locked. That didn't matter. After the confrontation at the Serendip, he expected only further trouble. His .44 was out, gripped steadily in his hand. He turned the key and then threw the door open, at the same time drawing back out into the corridor so that if an intruder opened fire he would escape injury.

But no hail of bullets greeted him, only the darkness of the room. Cautiously, he reached in, snapped on the light.

He'd been right. There was someone there. A man he recognized from the boat and the Leeward Cay. But he had intentions other than ambushing Harry. Instead, he was sitting complacently in the room's sole chair, his hands in full view so that Harry could see that he posed no threat to him. He was a rotund man with a pate gone bald underneath his hat. In the sweltering air sweat had begun to roll off his brow and he was now getting out a pink handkerchief to wipe it away.

That Harry kept the Magnum trained directly on him did not seem to either surprise or disconcert him. He probably expected it.

"You are a very careful man, Mr. Callahan. Or is it Balsam? It's so hard to know what to call you. My name is Chauney. Dave Chauney. I am, as you are probably aware, an associate of Mr. Braxton."

"Are you going to leave on your own or am I going to have to throw you out?"

"Please, Mr. Callahan. I have no doubt you could hurl me through this window before I knew what hit me, and I want to assure you I'm going to leave just as soon as I've delivered my message. I don't particularly relish the idea of facing a .44 Magnum all night."

"Let's hear it."

"Well, first, let me tell you Mr. Braxton was very impressed by your performance tonight."

155

"Performance?"

"He was trying to convince his guests that you were probably the best officer on the San Francisco police force. But to lay aside all doubts, he contrived a little demonstration. He would have been very disappointed if you had failed him."

Now Harry understood why Braxton had appeared so pleased.

Chauney was quick to add that the two men who'd accosted him were not let in on the scenario. "That wouldn't have been fair, would it?"

"That's the thing I like about your employer," Harry said. "His love of fairness."

"Mr. Braxton has given you a lot of thought," Chauney went on.

"I'm sure he has."

"And he's concluded that it makes no sense, the two of you being on opposite sides. He admires people who are resourceful and ambitious—and above all, successful."

"No one likes a loser, is that it?"

"You see, Mr. Braxton thinks you have style. There aren't many people in this world who have style." Chauney, as he continued talking, was growing more expansive, no longer mindful of the gun Harry held on him. "He would like to make you an offer to come work for him. Not as a bodyguard. He has more bodyguards than he knows what to do with. Nor would he make such an offer to you. It would be an insult, he knows that. No, he would want you to organize operations in San Francisco for us."

"What kind of operations are you talking about?" Harry shut the door to give them added privacy. He did not release his gun but he rested it. The best thing to do he decided was to draw this Chauney out as much as possible, pretend to be interested.

"Well, it's hard to say. This is something you have to speak to Mr. Braxton about. But I can tell you it

156

would be important work, strategic, and enormously rewarding. You could remain on in the police department. Actually, Mr. Braxton would prefer it that way."

"Like Sandy Patel?"

Chauney made a sound that was halfway between a cough and a chortle; perhaps it was a comment on the late Officer Patel. "He was a flunky, more trouble than he was worth. We had something far more important in mind for you. We're talking about the real political power of the city here. Not just the docks. The whole city. Just because Mr. Braxton was obliged to leave the country temporarily doesn't mean he's severed his connections with his supporters back home. Not by any means."

Harry was quiet.

"Well?" Chauney evidently thought he'd made his point. "If you're interested—and you don't have to give me a yes or no answer yet—we can set up a meeting between you and Mr. Braxton and—" His voice fell off abruptly.

"And?"

"I'm not sure I'm really authorized to tell you this. But tomorrow on the shuttle a friend of Mr. Braxton's is arriving. Someone from home. I mention it only because if you decide to join us he'll be the man you'll be working with."

Harry knew better than to ask Chauney his name but the blood was pounding in his temples. Although he was rarely excited, he nonetheless found it difficult to conceal his anticipation. But Chauney was so preoccupied with his sales pitch that he never noticed. Here at last, Harry thought, he would have the opportunity to discover who had set him up on so many occasions.

"So this meeting, where and when?"

Chauney had an incredulous look in his eyes. He'd probably been told that Harry would refuse and bodily throw him out, maybe worse. That Harry had actually expressed interest virtually shocked him into silence.

"Well?"

Chauney regained the use of his voice. "I don't know yet. But don't worry. It's a small island. We'll find you."

As Chauney moved toward the door—and he did this slowly, the heat seemed to have sapped him of any energy he might have had—he turned to give Harry a final piece of information. "I don't know whether you've guessed it yet, I suspect a man of your intelligence would have. But you really have no choice but to join us. That's the only way you're ever going to leave Tapaquite—alive at any rate."

Seventeen

As soon as it got to be morning, but before the sun ascended too high and caused the heat to become unbearable, Harry took himself down to the Plaza de Armas which was where the natives of Ocho Rios lingered; not in any expectation of finding employment, for there was none, but just to idle away the time in talk and unending consumption of coffee, beer, and home-brewed rum which burned the throat in its passage down to the gut.

The looks the natives gave Harry were withering; they did not especially care for people who were not born in Tapaquite. Their voluble chatter ceased abruptly as soon as Harry stepped into view. When Harry approached them—and there must have been forty or fifty of them congregating about a derelict cafe whose tables spilled over onto the potted pavement—they exchanged darkly significant glances. What's this cat want? they seemed to be saying, but only with their eyes, because they knew better than to speak in the presence of an intruder.

"Any of you fellows looking for work?" Harry addressed them, uncertain of what kind of response he was going to get.

One man stepped forward, spitting a wad of tobacco out in prelude to replying. "What work you talking about?"

"Fifteen dollars, U.S., a day for keeping track of some people."

"Keeping track of some people, huh?" the man repeated, eyeing Harry with increasing suspicion. "Fifteen dollars, U.S." He nodded. "Twenty dollars, U.S." Money matters were to be settled first, details of the job could come later.

"Eighteen," countered Harry. Already this was fifteen dollars above the normal wage on the island—if anyone could even get a job.

The man looked back to his companions. The offer evidently satisfied him. There was a low murmur, a kind of rustling chorus of agreement. "How many of us would you need, man?"

"Six. I'd need six for a couple of days."

Somehow six volunteers materialized. There was neither bickering nor fighting over which six; could be they'd figured out priorities in advance.

The spokesman now decided it might be wise to ascertain some of the specifices. "Who we to look out for?"

"A fellow lives over in Boca de la Sierpe. Him and all his friends."

"Braxton Mister?" the man asked.

"I see he's well known in these parts."

This information did not prove especially pleasing to any of these people. "You saying you want us to spy out over Boca way?"

"That's all I'm saying. Eighteen dollars just for watching who comes and goes from Boca and where they go." To Harry it seemed an easy task and he wondered at the darkening expressions on the faces before him.

The spokesman had in the meantime rejoined his circle and was now conferring with a couple of his companions. Finally he turned back to Harry, shaking his head vehemently. "Sorry, man, we no are going Boca way."

Thinking he might be holding out for additional

money Harry said he'd put up twenty per man. It made no difference.

"Braxton Mister, he—" And here he made a slashing motion across the base of his throat with his hand. "Twenty dollar, U.S., hundred dollar, U.S., what matter when you dead, man?"

The fear that these men suffered from was so palpable that Harry immediately gave up all idea of arguing with them; you could see it in their eyes. Braxton had been in Tapaquite for just about a week and already he had earned a reputation for inspiring terror. Several years had had to pass before he had achieved the same effect in San Francisco. He was getting better at it all the time.

If these impoverished men balked at opposing Braxton—or even being put in a situation where they *looked* as though they were—then Harry might just as well resign himself to one unhappy but inescapable fact: he was operating wholly on his own.

When he arrived back at the Crown, intending to sample the breakfast that was included in the room tariff, he found Chauney waiting for him, rocking back and forth in a wicker chair on the hotel's shabby veranda.

"Mr. Callahan, what a pleasure to see you."

"That's hard for me to imagine but we'll let it go."

"I've given Mr. Braxton an account of our conversation last night and he's mightily pleased by your interest. He proposes that we all get together down at the docks— right over there you can see it—oh, at about four this afternoon. Mr. Braxton is anxious to take you for a little cruise, show you the local fishing grounds."

Harry had hoped for a more public meeting, some place from which he could extricate himself if need be. A forty-foot sailboat, manned by Braxton's bodyguards, was not the public place he had in mind.

"Frankly, I'd like to postpone the pleasure cruise for another day. I was thinking more along the lines of the

161

Cay. That way I could just sit and look at the sea and not have to go out on it."

Chauncy frowned. "I'm afraid you don't understand, Mr. Callahan. Mr. Braxton's not offering you the choice of meeting places. Arrangements have been made." He got up from the chair, mopping his brow of all the sweat that had collected there. "See you at four."

Braxton's selection of four o'clock was no arbitrary decision. The shuttle plane would arrive from Fort-de-France at three, allowing more than enough time for the mystery guest from San Francisco to get into Ocho Rios from the airport.

Harry determined on going out to the airport himself to see who this visitor was in advance of his meeting. In fact, if he could identify him then, he wouldn't have to even risk the meeting at all.

At the very bottom of Crown Street Harry found a taxi, which was in slightly better shape than the one he'd taken the day before. He woke up the driver who looked quite astonished that someone should actually desire his services.

This driver was also less inclined to talk or play tourist guide, and so he was able to deliver Harry to the airport long before the shuttle plane was to come in.

At this drowsy time of day, when the sun was close to its zenith, the terminal was as desolate as a graveyard. Even the energetic little boys and wizened men who shrilly harangued newly arriving tourists could barely summon up the initiative to raise their heads and look at Harry.

But as the hour approached when the plane was due in, the terminal came to life. Beggars, taxi drivers, vendors, guides, and one customs official seemed to materialize from out of nowhere.

So did a number of very serious-looking fellows who stood out in uncomfortable jackets and slacks that were obviously inappropriate for this torrid heat. The way they

162

separated, taking up positions at different corners of the terminal, seemed to indicate that they thought themselves inconspicuous. But whatever else they were, they certainly weren't inconspicuous.

After several minutes had passed the faint droning rumble of the incoming Cessna registered in Harry's ears. Several others in the lounge also noticed it. Many hurried to the window to catch a glimpse of the plane, but Braxton's men—Harry knew the type well enough by now to identify them with no trouble whatsoever—stayed put. The expressions on their faces however altered subtly; they looked more worried now and their bodies were tensed, in readiness for action.

The Cessna was the same that Harry had arrived on, and its landing was as uncertain as yesterday's had been. It seemed to bounce as though it preferred being up in the air, then it settled down on the airstrip for good and began taxiing steadily in the direction of the terminal.

At that moment, from out of a barracks-like building that stood adjacent to the terminal a platoon of military personnel came running. They probably represented the only police force and army the small island had. They were armed with light carbines to which they'd fixed bayonets.

No sooner had the plane come to a full stop than the soldiers had taken up position directly beneath it. When the stairs were down the stewardess appeared at the open door and looked out. Then, with a nod, she descended. Following right behind were a group of men, all in somber suits, all with dark glasses, all carrying leather briefcases; they proceeded down the steps in a great hurry. The soldiers flanked them on both sides and, like an honor guard, accompanied them as they walked to the terminal.

It seemed that whomever Braxton's distinguished guest was, he had enough power to reserve the shuttle from Fort-de-France completely for himself and his party. Try as Harry might, he could not get a look at him. Nor was there much of an opportunity to do so. The customs official motioned them through without inspecting either their documents or the luggage which was brought in off the plane within minutes.

At this point the soldiers surrendered their charges to Braxton's men. There were a few polite words exchanged, a few obligatory handshakes, and then they headed en masse to the exit. Outside, three limousines stood waiting.

Harry kept trying to move in closer. The soldiers were not interested in him; their objective was to prevent the beggars, taxi drivers, and vendors from approaching. When someone proved too determined, the soldiers would glare and threaten to impale him with their bayonets. This action generally caused the person to withdraw.

But Harry did not look like a beggar, taxi driver, or vendor, and the way he was dressed, for all these soldiers knew, he might well be a member of Braxton's burgeoning group.

But while the soldiers more or less ignored him, Braxton's associates in plainclothes did not. For a time Harry had enjoyed perfect anonymity mostly because no one had expected to see him at the airport to begin with. But one of the men happened to recognize Harry and he was not especially happy about it. Particularly when he realized that Harry was coming dangerously close to Braxton's guest on whom this VIP service was being lavished.

In fact, Harry was so intent on seeing who it was that he momentarily let down his defenses. Three of the men who had stationed themselves at intervals about the lounge now came swooping down, determined to hustle Harry away as fast as they were able. They weren't certain whether Harry's interest lay in the new arrival or in catching the outgoing flight, but in neither case were they going to allow Harry to do what he planned.

It was only when they had circled around in behind him, using the imitation marble columns to protect themselves—for they had learned from experience that Harry was someone to reckon with—that Harry became aware he was in some degree of trouble. Facing him were maybe half a dozen men in uniforms—boys more than men, scarcely out of their teens. Behind him—well, he would have no idea until he turned around and he wasn't certain he wanted to do that yet.

But the choice was not his to make. One of the three, the bravest or the stupidest, it was hard to tell which, risked sacrificing his cover and moved into the open, not even bothering to be too quiet about this since he was convinced that the hubbub in the lounge would adequately drown out the sound of his footsteps. Harry had not yet made it known that he had recognized his predicament. The man was simply calculating his risks and gambling.

Sliding out a Baretta from a shoulder holster, the man drew to within ten feet of Harry, then raised his weapon so that if he fired—and this was not his intention—the back of Harry's head would be shattered.

He was about to call to Harry, to command him to disarm and submit himself into his custody, but right then an elderly man with shags of gray hair springing out of his scalp saw the gun, pointed to it, and shrieked, and in doing so alerted Harry. Another of Braxton's aides emerged from behind the column and, infuriated, brought the barrel of his gun down against the old man. Blood raced to the surface of his skin and with a sigh the beggar tumbled to the floor. There was suddenly a lot of screaming; panic rooted itself among the crowd and it began to eddy toward any means of egress.

With this unexpected distraction, Harry had time to maneuver. He submerged himself in the crowd, which was not easy to do because he was taller and whiter than those who surrounded him. Evidently he made for a target, however imperfect, because two bullets whined over his head. This only stirred the crowd to quicken their pace with the result that a few of the less nimble ones tripped and fell. Rather than stopping for them, people pressed on, trampling them.

Even though the limousines were pulling away with their passengers, the soldiers felt compelled to restore order. They hadn't any idea of who had fired the shots or why but they quickly went into action, crouching, bringing their carbines up to their shoulders, preparatory to laying down a barrage. Maybe they thought a revolution was underway.

Two of Braxton's men ran toward the exits, deciding that this would be the best tactic for heading off Harry's escape. But the fact of the matter was that Harry really couldn't escape, being stuck as he was in the midst of this thronging mass; every which way he turned, he was blocked off. There were more shots. It didn't make any sense why anyone should be shooting given just how confused the situation was. But the effect was to increase the panic. People were wailing and throwing themselves against the person in front of them in an attempt to extricate themselves.

The soldiers were now under the impression that they were confronting a full-scale attack and never mind if they couldn't determine from where exactly it was coming. Either their commanding officer gave the order to fire or else one of the men simply got too trigger happy and started shooting on his own. In any case, once it started no one was in any hurry to stop it.

To the right and left of him people were being flung back and forth by the force of the bullets, like so many kites in the wind, but because there was virtually no room to maneuver in, they could not fall. They remained trapped between other bodies, some living, some not, suspended grotesquely, blood pouring from them and forming small pools at their feet. The bullets cut through flesh, they cut through poles and posters advocating the virtues of the national lottery. Several pinged against the black board that displayed the time of day flights came in and left for Fort-de-France.

When the man in front of Harry—a toothless hawker of mangoes and nuts—was thrown aside by a round,

Harry suddenly found he could get free. Leaping over a corpse, he got himself to the outside, sprinting through the lounge to a place of safety.

He was spotted, not by one of Braxton's hirlings but by a soldier who evidently didn't like the idea of anyone escaping. He was not a very good shot; the bullets were way wide of the mark. Harry knew enough not to trust to luck, however, and he pivoted around, firing simultaneously. He'd not really aimed, he had an instinctive sense of where to shoot. And his aim bore out his instinct; the soldier's neck erupted in a spout of blood and he keeled right over, a vastly surprised and irritated expression on his face.

Another soldier turned his attention toward Harry, but by this time he had lost all advantage and he was hit before he could get off a shot. He stiffened at the shock and fell back partway, then, somehow, improbably raised himself again. With a shudder he began coughing. Blood flowed generously from his mouth, and then he collapsed again; obviously he was never going to move.

Seeing that the panic-stricken crowd that was busy stampeding toward the exit was not resisting them, the soldiers decided to concentrate on Harry. There were maybe ten of them—Harry was not sure where they'd all come from—and they spread out, hoping to encircle him and trap him in a withering fire. They no longer cared about the beggars and vendors who had broken the glass doors from their hinges in their attempt to get out of the terminal. Behind them they'd left several bodies—who'd finally been allowed the opportunity to crumple to the floor. Some were still alive and crying in pain; you could see them writhing, struggling to get back on their feet and walk away as if this alone could overcome the gaping holes in their bodies.

The strategy the soldiers had was clear; these were not West Point graduates Harry was dealing with. He realized that he could not allow them to fan out and so he fired off four rounds in rapid succession which, while not

167

doing any damage, did send the soldiers scurrying. They were unused to combat and would sooner hunker down than face someone who seemed to know what he was doing. Their hasty retreat allowed Harry time to put in another clip.

This abrupt interruption in the firefight left the soldiers confused. They couldn't even see Harry what with all the smoke; he must be behind one of the columns but which one they had no idea, not so long as he held his fire.

In another country there would have been reinforcements; you would have heard sirens heralding the arrival of a great deal more firepower. But this was Tapaquite, and there were no more reinforcements. This was the island's entire army. And it was all dedicated to one purpose—destroying Harry.

Whether Braxton's men had determined that they were unneeded in view of this situation or whether they thought it the better part of wisdom to escape before these ignorant soldiers turned their guns on *them* Harry didn't know. But one way or another, they seemed to have withdrawn.

Now a couple of the soldiers decided that it was worth venturing out; their comrades laid down a covering fire from behind what once had been the reservations desk. Not that it mattered. Having no real sense of where exactly Harry was, their fire was totally ineffective.

The problem for Harry was that he was denied access to the only two routes of escape available; one led out to the airstrip past the customs control, the other, with all its shattered glass, lay well within the line of sight of the soldiers. And true, though they might be inexperienced and badly trained and callow, their very amateurishness made them in some respects as dangerous as hardened troops. They might kill Harry just as dead. There was such a thing as beginner's luck. Harry was not at all inclined to be overconfident.

The two soldiers moving forward were obviously afraid; the fear showed in their eyes, sweat was visible on

168

their brows. They seemed to expect that they would be shot down at any moment and were surprised that they had survived so far. The others began to follow them, but they were very tentative. They looked puzzled, unable to figure out what had happened to Harry. Soon they were all exposed which was what Harry's intention had been.

Firing four rounds, he managed to score four hits. The first victim spun around, clinging to his ruptured stomach. The second went down in a heap so fast that it was impossible to see where the bullet had penetrated. The third was caught in motion; his thigh sustained the damage and on impact he was thrown up into the air like a marionette suddenly being jerked up offstage. The fourth was hit squarely in the chest. In his descent to the ground he fell against a companion and knocked him over, too. The survivor remained down, whether because he thought he'd been hit as well or because he simply decided it was a whole lot safer to do so.

This left just six men in action and none of them was happy with the way their ranks had so suddenly been decimated. They seemed to have lost all sense of direction—possibly their commanding officer had been put out of commission—and so rather than keep up the engagement, they scattered, falling back, some to where they'd hidden before—behind the reservations desk, others right out the door. Only one soldier, undaunted, remained to continue firing. At least he had a good idea of where Harry was. He yelled to his deserting comrades, calling them to come back, but they just weren't interested.

Throughout all this, the wounded people on the floor, their life ebbing away in their hemorrhaging blood, still were screaming, demanding an end to their agony.

Harry determined that it was either stay pinned down indefinitely or else risk exposing himself for a few moments while he sought cover closer to the exit out to the airstrip. It looked to him like he could attain it with one concentrated run of ten seconds' duration.

Hurtling himself out from behind the column that had afforded him his safety, he rushed, weaving in and out in the direction of the open door. The soldier's bullets followed him but failed to catch up with him. Instead they punctured significant portions of the walls and the glass windows which burst apart into thousands of fragments.

Harry was already outside and nearing the tarmac when the soldier, disgusted, picked himself up and charged after him.

As fast as Harry was running he noticed that two of the fleeing soldiers were running faster—and away from the terminal. Their carbines lay discarded on the steamy asphalt surface.

The soldier found himself a new position from which to continue firing; he seemed to feel that it was worth the trouble since Harry had no shelter available to him— there was just lots of open space on the airstrip and Harry presented a clear target. However, the lone soldier appeared not to have noticed what kind of shelter he'd selected or else noticing, hadn't considered it the liability it was. Because he was now directly behind a rack that held two unwieldy fuel tanks. And while he couldn't be seen it made no difference to Harry who turned and still in motion, fired the last two rounds in the Magnum at the tanks.

Instantly the tanks exploded; there was a huge roar and a ball of flame shot up toward the pale blue sky. The soldier's scream was lost in this roar; the force of the explosion blew him apart, sending bits and pieces of him into the air. A scorched hand dropped down not far from where Harry stood watching the spectacle.

In the distance there was the sound of a high-pitched siren. Most likely it was the island's one available ambulance; there was only one available hospital too, a two-story structure crumbling inside and out, and there was no question it was unprepared for a catastrophe of this nature.

It was strange, Harry considered, to find himself alone on this airstrip. But there certainly was no sense lingering about here. He determined on finding a taxi—if there was anyone left to drive one—and going back to the hotel. He glanced at his watch. After four. Well, he had missed his meeting with Braxton and his guest from the States. Under the circumstances, this was probably a good thing.

By the time dusk fell Harry was becoming nervous. Not that anything had happened to him since his own flight from the airport. That was the problem. When nothing happened it made Harry edgy. Dinner at the Whitby. Drinks at the Cay. Another drink at the Mimoso. A periodic reconnaissance of the pier. And nowhere was there a sign of Braxton, his boat, or his men.

Like they'd been night, the streets were relatively quiet. Except for the occasional tourist on his way from one bar to the other no one else was about; all the natives seemed to have melted into the tropical breezes that swept in from the Caribbean at night. The people who wanted to sell you bananas and lottery tickets and the beggars who cursed you even when you gave them some money, all of them had vanished.

Harry concluded that there was nothing more he was going to get done—nothing more that he could do actually—this night. He decided to return to his hotel room and get some sleep—that was if he didn't have to contend with another intruder who had a speech to deliver to him.

Two blocks away from the Crown, a figure stepped out from the shadows, partially blocking Harry's way. Immediately, Harry was on the alert. Streetlighting being as minimal as it was in Ocho Rios, it was difficult to make out what this man looked like from a distance. Still, Harry recognized a threatening situation and he stepped back, withdrawing into the shadows while he lifted out a fully reloaded Magnum from underneath his jacket.

The man approached him. He was now close enough for Harry to discern him with greater clarity. He had seen him before, no doubt of that, and just last night. He was one of the assailants who'd unwittingly participated in Braxton's little scenario.

Just as he was wondering what had happened to his

friend, the one with the blowgun, he heard a faint whis-pery noise, almost like a sigh. He half-turned in response but just then felt a sharp, violent pain in his left leg. A small dart quivered in the wound. Well, he thought as the drug sped through his blood to his brain, he didn't have to wonder any longer. Darkness took hold of him before he reached the ground.

Eighteen

Shadows, hazy and shapeless, began gradually to form themselves into something more coherent. Recovering consciousness Harry found to be an exacting task, a violent struggle to draw up to the light. But when he got to the light and opened his eyes he didn't like what he found there.

Looming over him was Matt Braxton, and he was surrounded by the men who had grown tan and prosperous over the years following him and doing his bidding. Harry realized after a while that he was in a room, and not a very big one, with stucco walls all of white; and there were no windows.

"How are you feeling, Mr. Callahan?"

Braxton spoke to him like a man truly concerned over the state of his health. He gazed down at Harry and his face, capturing all of Harry's visual field, assumed monstrous proportions: big inquisitive gray eyes studying him.

"Like shit," Harry replied. Small rocks seemed to be bouncing back and forth, hard, against the walls of his skull.

"You'll recover. The drug wears off in an hour or so." Braxton pulled over a hassock and seated himself next to Harry's bed. "That was some stunt you pulled at the airport." Braxton shook his head gravely but kept his slightly idiotic smile fixed on his lips. "I don't know what

173

you were doing there, I surely hope it wasn't with intention
tious to leave, but it was not a wise thing to do. Mr
Chauney invited you to a little party I was having or
board my boat and you didn't come. I was insulted, I wa
truly hurt. Well, it can't be helped ...." He glanced back
at the men gathered around him, maybe to see if they
were still attending to his every word. "Mr. Chauney tol
you that I was interested in acquiring your services.
figured you to be a reasonable man who recognizes wher
the odds are against him. I wanted to give you a chance
Truth is I like you, Callahan. I mean I hate you, but
respect you and that's important. To a simple uneducated
guy like me, respect's what counts in this life. Don't you
agree?" Getting no answer, he continued. "I assume you
agree. So I said to myself, Matt, this cop, he could prove
useful. Give him some money, we're talking big bucks
he's got instinct, he's got intelligence ... What I'm saying
Mr. Callahan, me not being so good with words, is tha
you have a choice. Most people deal with me, I never give
them no choice. You, you're different. I'll give you ar
hour. You mull it over. You come join my crew, you'l
never regret it. You don't, in an hour you'll be in the
bottom of the water out there." He motioned toward the
wall, perhaps expecting to find a window. "I may be a
hard man but I'm an honest one. This is square business."

He kept pausing, waiting for Harry to respond, to
react in some way. But Harry didn't. He could barely
concentrate on what Braxton was saying; he was too busy
trying to fight back the pain that had taken up residence
in his head.

"And don't think you can simply say yes and go
back to San Francisco and forget about it. We don'
operate that way. We do a deal we do a deal. But you're
locked into it. We get your signature on a few papers, we
make photos, document some transactions. All for our
own protection, you understand? If nothing goes wrong
you got nothing to fear. We put our records in a very safe
place. If not, then, hey, we're not responsible. The way

we work it is first we fuck you, then we kill you. Nothing personal, it's just the way we work it."

"I get you," said Harry, not really interested in the mechanics of this.

"I want you to meet a friend of mine, a fellow who can verify what I'm telling you." He gestured toward the door behind him. A guard opened it and a man walked in.

Harry knew immediately that this was the visitor who'd been shuttled away from the airport too fast, and under too much protection, for him to get a glimpse of. And he knew that this same man had acted as the broker and rabbi for Braxton back in San Francisco. He'd met him before.

It was the assistant D.A.—Robert Nunn. He looked as smug as ever. He offered a smile to Harry.

"It's strange," he said, "how we keep running into each other."

"Yeah, and in the oddest places, too."

"You might be confused, Mr. Callahan, seeing my friend, Bob Nunn, here." To make it clear just what good friends they were, Braxton clapped his hand on the assistant D.A.'s back. "Oh sure, we once were on opposite sides, but things, as you know, change. We used to work with Pritchard, Bob's boss, but people get old. Pritchard's on his way out. And frankly, Pritchard was too close to Bull and you know what they say when you add up one shark and one fluke. You get one shark!" He had a good laugh at this. His friends apparently felt that it wouldn't hurt if they joined in laughing as well. "Pritchard and Bull, they used to spend hours eating together. Places like the Top of the Mark. And you know who paid for all those meals?" Braxton stabbed his chest with a spatulated thumb. "I did. Out of my fucking pocket. Thirty bucks, forty bucks a meal, it ain't much. But you add it up over the years. Hey, it gets goddamn expensive." He was really serious about this; the thought of all the money he'd laid out over the years for Bull's benefit and for Pritchard made him furious. Then he stopped himself, realizing he'd gotten distracted. The smile reappeared. "Sorry. Bull's a sore subject with me. One of these days, if we ever find the son of a bitch, I'm going to have him sent down here for a little heart-to-heart. So now we come to my friend Mr. Nunn here. Bob, well, he fucked me but good. See, but do I hold it against him?" Another laugh straight up from the belly which had become quite big with all the food he was consuming on Tapaquite. "We get along just like brothers now." Weirdly, Nunn didn't look at all embarrassed about this. On the contrary, he seemed almost pleased. "It's just like what I told you, Mr. Callahan, I don't hold no grudges. I see talent, I use it. That's how I got to where I am today. That's why I'm never down for long. Talent's for me or against me, makes no difference. I buy it or I dispense with it. That's how it works with us."

"That's what you keep telling me."

"Harry, he's right," Nunn put in, giving his testimonial. "It makes sense in a lot of ways."

"That's what they taught you in law school?"

"Don't turn nasty now," Braxton said. "I've given you an hour." He looked down at his Seiko. "And we've already eaten into that time with our jabbering. So you begin doing some serious thinking and we'll leave you in peace."

He signaled his retainers that they were to exit. On the way out Harry called to Nunn. "You know what they say about lawyers, don't you?"

Nunn shook his head. "No, Harry, what do they say?"

"Comes the revolution they'll shoot them all first."

Nunn wouldn't answer that, and so he turned and went away with all the rest of them. The metal door clanged shut. Then a bolt was flipped into place.

The problem now was—aside from facing a death sentence—Harry had no way to determine when his hour was up; along with everything else his captors had seized, they'd taken his watch.

After thoroughly checking the room, Harry soon

176

ascertained that there was no way he was going to escape, not with the walls a couple of feet thick, as he estimated them, not with no window. Nor was there available any instrument, even the homiest of household objects—a pot, for instance—that he could employ in defending himself. If you had to stay too long in this room, with its bare cold white walls, Harry considered, you were liable to go mad. He had less than an hour. Still it was not the sort of place he would have chosen to await his execution.

It could have been just a couple of minutes that had passed for all Harry knew. Seemed in any case like a whole lot longer. In this sensory deprivation environment, minutes had a way of taking hours to go by. But whatever time had elapsed it was obvious to Harry that his hour was not up. Nonetheless, there was a terrible racket at the door. It didn't last long. Sounded like chalk being scraped against a blackboard. Whatever it was it sent chills up Harry's back.

The bolt now was being unlatched. He positioned himself by the side of the door—the right side—waiting to grab hold of whomever came in and throw him to the floor. It was, he felt, his only chance. Undoubtedly, he'd confront a regiment of armed men but better to take that risk than to allow himself to be dragged away unresisting and garroted, then hurled into the shimmering waters of the Caribbean.

The door came open and as it did so a man came with it. There was no need for Harry to try to subdue him. Someone had already done it for him. The guard collapsed at Harry's feet, his gun pitching from him at the same time. At first it was difficult to account for his condition until Harry noticed the small, perfectly round red hole that appeared in the middle of his forehead.

The dead man was followed into the room by the person who'd made him that way. Another old friend from the past. Looking frazzled maybe, a bit more haggard, but easily identifiable: Darlene Farley.

She entered the room, a .38 in her hand, ignoring the

body lying at her feet. Baffled, she looked around for Harry, clearly unaware he was standing directly behind her. Harry was a bit puzzled, too, speculating on this crazy lady's motives—had she come to kill him? Well, that didn't make any sense. No reason to go out of her way to do that with his being condemned already.

Still, he took no chances and, grabbing her from behind, gripped her arms so that she was incapable of using her gun. She let out a small cry of surprise, twisted her neck to get a glimpse of Harry, muttered first, "Hey, you're hurting me," then, "I was looking for you. I came to help you."

Harry loosened but did not relinquish his grip. "And why's that?"

"We don't have much time. They'll come down here in a minute. Let me go. We've got to go find him."

She was talking a mile a minute; she talked like she smoked actually, starting a new word when she hadn't finished with the one before.

Harry moved her away from the door, then leaned down to retrieve the Baretta that had belonged to the guard. Only when he was armed did he allow her to go free.

The hallway, which he caught sight of for the first time, was empty as far as the eye could see. Empty and soundless.

"Calm down. Now who do we have to find?"

There was no way on earth this woman was going to calm down. No, she was flushed; her rage was a wonder to behold, the way it inflamed her eyes and set her lips trembling.

"Braxton, the fucker," she answered, spitting out his name. "I got a telegram from him three days ago. He told me he wanted me back. I came back and what do you suppose he did?"

Harry could guess. But he didn't have to.

"Soon as I got down here he treated me like shit. Wouldn't let me out of this goddamn place. Took off to town with his whores and his flunkies, wouldn't let me go

178

with them. Just wanted to teach me a lesson, he said. Well, OK, he wants to play it that way. I'll teach *him* a lesson!"

So this is how it is, Harry thought. Every time the girl gets pissed at her old man she comes to my rescue. This is one hell of a way to break a case.

In her fury she seemed almost to have forgotten Harry nor did she show any sign that she was now worried about the danger they faced.

"Where is Braxton?"

"Upstairs. They're all upstairs except for the bastards on the grounds. They told me you were down here. I said to myself, 'Shit, damned if old Matt ain't gonna be surprised to see Harry walking free.'" She giggled like a little girl. An insane little girl. And here Harry had thought he'd merely been dealing with a neurotic; well, it appeared that instead she was really quite far gone.

As she turned to continue her vendetta against her erstwhile lover, she tripped against the guard's corpse. In anger she kicked him irrelevantly in the ribs. Then she regained her composure. With a certain tinge of sadness to her voice she said, "I wasn't going to kill him. I don't want to kill anybody. Just was going to scare him a little. He didn't want to scare, that's all." She shrugged.

"It happens," Harry said, putting his hand on her shoulder, gently so as not to disconcert her further, and guided her out the door. The hallway, with its surface of flat white stone lit by shots of light pouring in through rows of windows, still remained empty. But no longer soundless. Footsteps echoed loudly off the stucco walls. Nonetheless, Harry and Darlene continued a bit farther; by tacit agreement they kept their steps quiet.

They'd scarcely progressed down the hallway when the shadow of a man—and judging by the shadow, a very tall man—fell across the foyer. Harry held back, flattening himself against the wall, but he was not in time to restrain Darlene, who in her headlong rush to get to Braxton had failed to notice the threat. When Harry threw his hand against her lips and attempted to plant her against the

179

wall alongside him she bit into his palm and gave a small shriek of surprise. She wasn't very good at getting hints.

The man heard her. He wasn't alarmed, merely curious. He peered down the hallway but what he saw first was the absence of any guard outside the door. Only then did he spot Darlene and Harry, but this had necessitated venturing farther down the hallway. By this point he was facing two guns whereas his hands were empty.

"Drop," Harry commanded him.

The man seemed not to know what he was talking about.

"To the floor. Down on the floor."

The man was paralyzed. He looked from Darlene to Harry and back again, then he bolted, hoping that they wouldn't fire or that he'd reach the staircase before they did.

"Oh no you don't!" Darlene cried, raising her .38 with both hands and firing it with astonishing precision before Harry could stop her.

The man kept going; you might have thought Darlene had missed. But it was only sheer momentum that carried him forward. Suddenly he seemed to realize that he'd been mortally wounded and so he simply stretched out his arms and keeled over, reluctantly obeying Harry's instruction.

It was at this point that Harry recognized exactly what kind of liability Darlene presented. No way to control her. No way to persuade her that the better part of wisdom was to escape the compound here at Boca de la Sierpe and live to fight another day. No, she was hellbent on exacting revenge against Braxton for all the real and imagined grievances she'd suffered at his hands and nothing was going to stop her.

As for Harry, his first priority was to get away, recoup, and consider his next strategy. But it became readily apparent that he was going to be denied that opportunity. Darlene, having neglected to use a gun equipped with a silencer, had by shooting this man alerted others upstairs. The guard she'd shot at close quarters and the sound of the shot had been muffled. But not this time. The report would have been heard throughout the villa.

There were footsteps coming down the stairs, and voices, and Harry knew now that there would be no escape without a struggle. Roughly, he pushed Darlene back out of the line of fire. He did not especially like the gun he had to work with, but in situations like this you took what was available.

It was not as easy for him to maneuver as it usually was; the drug still hadn't altogether worn off and there was a persistent fuzziness in his brain that wouldn't go away. He had to concentrate when he sighted his gun; it didn't come as natural to him as it usually did.

But even so he achieved his mark. The security man who first appeared took a round in his chest; it knocked him off-balance but not down and he tottered several moments, his own gun discharging ineffectually, puncturing out holes in the ceiling and dislodging chunks of plaster which rained down on him. But the time he took in dying gave the others behind him a chance to descend the stairway in safety—Harry couldn't get a line on them to fire.

Darlene was directly behind him, but rather than cowering under the hail of bullets, she enthusiastically threw herself into the battle, loosing a steady barrage in the direction of the attackers although to what effect it was hard to say. Harry had no opportunity to see to her, being as preoccupied as he was, but he hoped that when she'd exhausted her supply of ammunition she would drop back and withdraw from the conflict. No such luck. She'd been far-sighted enough, even in her madness—perhaps because of it—to carry additional cartridges, which she dug out of her handbag.

Because Braxton's men could not fall back without sacrificing their advantage, they decided that their only real alternative was to rush Harry and Darlene, assuming that by their very number they would overwhelm them.

In their forefront Harry noticed the man who'd

181

brought him down with the blowgun. In this instance, however, he had discarded his favorite weapon for an FN automatic which with his good hand he aimed at Harry. But he was moving so fast that his shot went awry, gouging out a thick wad of stucco. Whether it was Darlene's shot or Harry's was less significant than the fact that someone managed to hit him, driving him back in the direction the bullet had taken. The FN clattered to the floor. He couldn't hold it when he had his open stomach to attend to. His mouth opened, he seemed to be trying to speak though no words emerged. Then, with a darkening look on his face, he sank to his knees. He didn't go down any farther, just stayed that way, on his knees like a penitent, clutching his stomach, waiting to see whether or not he would die. A second man—Harry recognized him from the airport—had a better aim and his rounds were digging up patches of stone mere inches from where Darlene and Harry were spread out. But again he was exposed, and in his attempt to close the distance between them he threw aside his caution with the result that he was hurled back, like his friend the blowgunner, taken off his feet by a bullet—probably fired by Darlene—that shattered his kneecap and in its upward trajectory lodged somewhere in the muscles of his thigh. As he fell he jostled another assailant, causing him to lose his momentum; before he could recover Harry took him out with a round that, impacting above his heart, spun him around twice before dropping him to the ground.

There were two others right behind but recognizing how futile their initial strategy had been, they withdrew—or tried to anyway—clambering back up the stairs. But to do this successfully they had to turn, and in turning they lost valuable moments. Harry sprang up, with Darlene following right behind him, and raced to the foot of the stairs, firing as he went. One man clumsily stumbled right into the path of a bullet that otherwise would have done no harm. It passed through his head, entering at the tip of his spine and exiting right underneath his left eye. The exit wound was large; it had to be if it was to accommodate the amount of blood, brain tissue, and chips of bone that went flying through it. Much of the bloody material was spewed over his colleague, hitting him smack in the face so that he was temporarily blinded, his eyes misted by the blood and the gelatinous substance that had once done the thinking and dreaming for the man who lay spread-eagled on the stairs. In such circumstances, to be temporarily blinded was to invite permanent blindness. Darlene was much more exhilarated by this firefight than Harry; and being miraculously immune from bullets as some irrationally self-confident people occasionally are, she gave no thought to climbing up the stairs and putting her .38 to the survivor's head and pulling the trigger. At such close proximity she was almost knocked over by the force of the recoil. The man obligingly flipped over the railing and smashed to the stone floor. Smoke thickened in the air, mixed with the stench of blood and cordite.

The stairs were slick with blood and unidentifiable viscera. Men were coming through the front door now and there were others appearing at the head of the stairs. This placed Harry and Darlene in the particularly unenviable position of being caught between the two groups. No choice but to keep firing—first down, then up.

Harry chose to advance up; retreat was out of the question now. He kept low and Darlene followed his example. The confusion and the smoke lent them a certain advantage. For one thing, the newly arriving security force wasn't precisely sure what was happening or who their targets were supposed to be.

And by keeping low the way they were doing, Harry and Darlene invited fire from those positioned at the top. One bullet caught Harry in the fleshy part of his right arm but he felt no pain. Another grazed Darlene's lovely stockinged leg but she too didn't seem to register its impact. But many of the bullets flew inches above them, continuing on so that they struck a couple of the men who'd just come into the hallway below. The result of this was that now the security men in the hallway began aiming higher up, mistakenly believing that they were under fire from their own allies.

"Aim for their feet!" Harry whispered to Darlene which was what she did because that's all she could see from where she was. They could see where they'd hit— the blood spurting from the row of anonymous ankles— and they could hear the cries of pain which followed almost immediately.

They succeeded in putting an abrupt end to the opposition from above. By the time they reached the top landing they found themselves in a sea of tangled flailing limbs. Men were crawling in all directions, resembling a colony of ants whose hill has just been flattened by a boot heel. Blood, streaming out of several wounds, collected and oozed in ever larger amounts down the stairs.

While there was still the occasional shot in their direction, whoever was firing seemed to have lost his fervor for the business. In any case, no one was pursuing them up the stairs; the bodies littering the immediate vicinity provided abundant testimony to the folly of doing that.

Ahead of Harry and Darlene was another hallway; this one was shorter and it terminated at a white door with a bronze handle to it.

"He'll be in there," Darlene said.

She was pale but unafraid; her eyes were deader than the men who lay at her feet. She was so intent on Braxton that nothing else mattered; not all this mayhem certainly, it might not have made the slightest impression on her.

"You don't think he might have gotten away?"

She shook her head. Her blonde hair was matted with blood though she was oblivious to this too. "There's a terrace adjoining the room through there, it's the only way. You'd have to jump down into the pool. That's not Matt's style. Oh no, you'll see, he won't run from a personal challenge. From a prison maybe. But not from you. He thinks he can still kill you."

"And what about you?"

She looked coldly at Harry and shrugged but didn't answer. Instead she began in the direction of the white door. Harry, more cautiously, trailed along a foot or so in back of her.

Grasping hold of the brass handle, she tugged at it and drew the door open. Harry had expected it to be locked. But as soon as he saw that it wasn't he threw himself against the nearest wall, preparing for the fire he assumed would come. But there was no fire.

Darlene sauntered in as though she were returning from a shopping excursion, the .38 held dramatically in her hand.

Harry, with his expropriated Baretta, stepped in after her.

It was a large and airy room. To one side was a canopied bed with a mirror overhead so that you could see just what sort of progress you were making under the covers—or on top of them. Directly opposite them was the terrace that Darlene had mentioned. And standing there, looking very uncomfortable, was Robert Nunn. He had a gun in his hand, but from the bewildered, slightly irritated expression on his face Harry could see that he wasn't anxious to use it—if in fact he knew how. Every so often he glanced down below the terrace to where the haven of the pool was presumably situated. Probably contemplating his chances if he jumped.

To the left was a large walnut desk whose top was strewn with papers and open books—law books in which Braxton had been researching in his quest for loopholes. But then Braxton was always a man on the lookout for loopholes. The man himself was standing right in back of the desk, his face a shade redder than usual perhaps but otherwise no different. He appeared not at all disturbed by the loss of so much of his security force. Nor was he going to allow Harry—or Darlene for that matter—the satisfaction of panicking or pleading for a truce.

Darlene kicked the door shut behind her. Her eyes

were locked on Braxton. She was not even remotely conscious of Nunn's presence.

"This is where it ends, Matt," she declared.

He only offered her a smile in return. "Darlene, Darlene," he said in a soothing voice that only infuriated her more. "There's no need to do this. So you've fallen for Callahan. It happens. Women do strange things for the men they love. I can understand that."

She threw her head back and laughed. "What are you talking about, Matt? You think I did it because I was in love with him?" She gave Harry a derisive glance. Which didn't bother Harry at all. Anyone who took on a lover like Darlene deserved what he got, Harry thought.

Darlene's hysterical reaction didn't trouble Braxton at all. His only interest was in disarming her and Harry. "Well then, we're in agreement. Mr. Callahan can be dispensed with."

Harry's fate didn't concern Darlene at all. "Who the hell cares. You're the problem, Matt. You fucked with me once too often."

All this while Harry kept looking down toward Braxton's hands. Only one was exposed to view, resting on the desk. The other he figured was grasping a gun. An important observation.

Nunn he worried less about. Nunn was more interested in the distance he was going to have to jump than in turning his gun on either Harry or Darlene. Obviously the exchange between Braxton and Darlene was getting on his nerves. Who loved whom, who fucked with whom; what possible difference did it make when you were staring death in the face?

"This wasn't supposed to happen like this, Matt," he said.

Braxton shrugged. "You're telling me." For the first time he regarded Harry directly. "Got farther than you thought, didn't you? Got farther than I thought too. Unfortunate. Because we could have made some kind of team, you and me."

At that moment he brought up his gun—actually it was Harry's, his .44 Magnum—thinking he had the advantage of surprise. But Harry had already fired two shots into him before he could pull the trigger, by which time it no longer mattered. Blood appeared at two points a couple of inches apart on his blue silk shirt and spread with astonishing speed until the wounds were indistinguishable. Braxton looked down at the blood with great puzzlement. His brow knotted and his hand groped tentatively for where the bullets had penetrated. Only when the blood was in his palm did he seem to understand what had happened. His eyes rolled up in his head and then he slid, slowly, with surprising gentleness, down below the desk.

It was only then that Darlene and Nunn reacted. That Braxton could be proven mortal was such a shock that they each needed time to absorb the event. Darlene whipped around, her eyes blazing, her lips like a red gash on her face. "You fucker! You killed him! You killed him!" Whether she hadn't wanted Braxton dead in the first place, in spite of all her avowels to the contrary, or whether she felt deprived of the revenge that should have been by rights hers, Harry wasn't sure—nor was he interested.

Darlene brought her gun around and fired—but as she did so, Harry turned aside, narrowly missing the bullet meant for him. There was another shot—and that, too, had been meant for him. Only Nunn, who had fired it, was not at all proficient with a pistol, and instead of hitting Harry he'd struck Darlene instead.

The look of surprise on her face was wonderous to behold. The bloodstain spread from a point near the sternum. Her breasts heaved with the pain of taking in breath. But the anger hadn't gone away. She did something that resembled a pirouette and studied Nunn, trying perhaps to make out his reasons for the attack.

Nunn, horrified by what he'd done, tried to back away, though this was impossible since he was already at the terrace's edge. He dropped his gun as though this gesture would signal his peaceful intentions.

"I didn't mean . . . I didn't mean . . ." he began, his face erupting with sweat, his glasses fogging with moisture. "It was for him, Darlene, I swear."

Such assurances in her dying moments meant nothing to Darlene, and she fired until there was nothing left in the chamber. Nunn's body vibrated like a tuning fork with each additional shot he took. One bullet shattered his glasses and continued straight on through his eye, putting a certain end to what would have been undoubtedly a promising, if somewhat corrupt, law career. He slumped down after that, having no life left in him to keep himself in anything like a vertical position.

Darlene, had the pain not been what it was, might have thought to save a bullet or two for Harry because certainly she had it in mind to kill him, too. But all she could do was to click the empty .38 over and over again. She nodded with satisfaction at seeing Nunn dead, then gradually turned to face Harry. "Oh, you're a shit," she said. With each word she uttered more blood perched on the edge of her lips. She closed her eyes, opened them again, saying, "Light's all gone, isn't it?" Then she flopped down at Harry's feet.

Now Harry heard the sound of men racing down the hall immediately outside the door. "Matt!" they were calling. "Are you in there, Matt?" Even at this point so late in the game they were reluctant to enter the inner sanctum without permission.

Harry had no intention of fighting off yet another regiment of gunmen. Everyone's luck ran out sometime. So he rushed out to the terrace and looked down. There was the pool all right. Swim to the end of it, clamber up and run, and you'd be lost in a thick undergrowth. Safety beckoned there.

The knocking continued, louder, more insistent. Someone was pulling on the handle. Harry turned, fired twice at the door. There was a loud groan in response. Harry had won himself a few moments' time. Since he did not share the late Robert Nunn's compunctions about diving into the pool, Harry balanced himself precariously on the railing and jumped.

A beautifully executed dive into the blue.

MEN OF ACTION BOOKS

DIRTY HARRY
By Dane Hartman

He's "Dirty Harry" Callahan—tough, unorthodox, no-nonsense plainclothesman extraordinaire of the San Francisco Police Department... Inspector #71 assigned to the bruising, thankless homicide detail ...A consummate crimebuster nothing can stop—not even the law! Explosive mysteries involving racketeers, murderers, extortioners, pushers, and skyjackers; savage, bizarre murders, accomplished with such cunning and expertise that the frustrated S.F.P.D. finds itself without a single clue; hair-raising action and violence as Dirty Harry arrives on the scene, armed with nothing but a Smith & Wesson .44 and a bag of dirty tricks; unbearable suspense and hairy chase sequences as Dirty Harry sleuths to unmask the villain and solve the mystery. Dirty Harry—when the chips are down, he's the most low-down cop on the case.

MEN OF ACTION BOOKS

THE HOOK
By Brad Latham

"The Hook" is William Lockwood, ace insurance investigator for Transatlantic Underwriters—a man whose name derives from his World War I boxing exploits, whose hallmark is class, whose middle name is violence, and whose signature is sex. In the late 1930s, when law enforcement was rough-and-tumble, The Hook is the perfect take-charge man for any job. He combines legal and military training with a network of contacts across America who honor his boxing legend. He's a debonair man-about-town, a bachelor with an awesome talent for women—and a deadly weapon in one-on-one confrontations. Crossing America and Europe in pursuit of perpetrators of insurance fraud, The Hook finds himself in the middle of organized crime, police corruption, and terrorism. The Hook—gentleman detective with a talent for violence and a taste for sex.